The villa they were touring had been built by the Crusaders . . .

"How about a picture of you?" James asked Lisa. He waved toward the arched doorway of the villa. "Stand over there—that way I can get some of the stonework of the background." He remained immobile for a minute then lowered the camera. "Damn . . . this thing's jammed. The release button doesn't work."

A frown creased her forehead. "The safety must still be on." She started toward him. "I'll show you how to release it."

There was a sudden whoosh of sound behind her and a thud jarred the earth under her feet. She shied like a skittish colt as she whirled to see what had happened.

A watermelon-sized boulder had fallen in the spot where she had stood a moment before. "My lord," she whispered in horror.

"Get away from here." James was in front of her, kneeling to survey the jagged-edged rock. "He might still be there," he muttered and turned to enter the arched doorway.

"No!" For the life of her, Lisa couldn't have said whether her sharp cry of protest was premeditated. All she knew was that she simply could not permit James to disappear into that suddenly sinister recess . . .

TREASURE OF THE HEART

by
Glenna Finley

A SIGNET BOOK
NEW AMERICAN LIBRARY
TIMES MIRROR

For Duncan

SIGNET, SIGNET CLASSICS, MENTOR, PLUME AND MERIDIAN BOOKS
are published by The New American Library, Inc.,
1301 Avenue of the Americas, New York, New York 10019

FIRST PRINTING, JUNE, 1971

12 13 14 15 16 17 18

PRINTED IN THE UNITED STATES OF AMERICA

"The human heart has hidden treasures,
In secret kept, in silence sealed—"

—Charlotte Brontë

CHAPTER ONE

By rights, that afternoon in Venice should have been one of those sleepy spring days that caused scattered tourists to bask happily in the balmy air and send silent thanks to their travel agents, who were slogging through the rain at home.

Bright sunshine illuminated the clear Italian sky and poured generously on the pigeons strutting about the Piazza San Marco, the only natives stirring, for the shops bordering the square were still shuttered for the siesta hours.

Near the Doge's Palace, two men lounged at an outdoor restaurant table enjoying their cappuccinos amid the quiet of their surroundings, a quiet broken only by the flutter of the birds' wings and the yawns of their waiter. A few yards away, a stray female tourist window-shopped before a deserted glove store display case.

The only thing out of keeping with the serenity of the mood was the expression on the face of the younger man, a rugged-looking individual in his early thirties. As he leaned forward to stare absently at the froth on the top of his coffee, his expression was that of a surly grizzly bear roused from hibernation by a nagging toothache.

"I don't like it, Adam," he was saying to his companion, "I don't like it at all! Good lord, imagine an assignment to play Boy Scout to a lady archaeologist for two weeks. If that isn't scraping the bottom of the barrel on the duty roster, I don't know what is."

His companion, a tall, spare man of forty-five, gave him a wry look. "Stop griping, Jim. You were chosen for this jaunt because of your background."

"Keeping tabs on a diplomaed gravedigger for a Mediterranean cruise!" The coffee was given a violent stir. "Don't you believe it. Why didn't they get the shore patrol or hire somebody from an escort service? Why get a lawyer?"

"Because the government preferred one James McAllister, Lieutenant, senior grade, United States Naval Reserve, who once spent a summer in the Mideast on an archaeological dig."

"Only because I was dating a blonde who was secretary to the professor in charge of the excavation," McAllister pointed out.

"I know that, but unfortunately your State Department doesn't."

"Just as I thought," Jim McAllister sat up straighter and pointed his coffee spoon accusing-

8

ly at the other man. "I should have seen your fine Canadian hand in this, Adam."

Adam Thorson refused to be ruffled. "How could a dreary professor of archaeology on sabbatical leave in England throw any weight around? You've been out in the sun too much, my boy."

"Don't 'my boy' me, you fraud. It was a sad day when I went to law school on your campus. I suppose it's just coincidence that you're planning to cruise the eastern Mediterranean on the same ship?"

Thorson seemed engrossed in a hunt for his pipe, which eventually emerged from the pocket of a rumpled blazer. "I imagine everything will be explained to us in time."

McAllister ran an impatient hand through his sun-streaked sandy hair and snorted with exasperation. "All this fuss over some missing jewelry. It's a waste of the taxpayers' money."

"That may be," the other said mildly, "but referring to that treasure as 'missing jewelry' is like calling the Hope Diamond a pretty bauble. At any rate, Miss Halliday will give us the final instructions when we meet on board the *Lucarno* tonight."

"Ah yes . . . our esteemed lady of the tombs." Jim slumped back down in his chair and glared at the back of the unsuspecting tourist who was still perusing the gloves on display. As he surveyed her trim ankles and a pair of truly admirable legs, awareness flared in his masculine glance. He looked questioningly over at Adam who merely shook his head slowly but definitely.

The younger man sighed. "It's a damn shame we're going to be here such a short time."

"Getting back to the subject of your harangue," Thorson said, "I wasn't aware that you knew Miss Halliday."

"I don't. Can you imagine my knowing anybody with a handle like Elisaveta Bowen Halliday? Just the name makes you think of bifocals and green soap."

"You're probably doing the woman an injustice."

"I doubt it." McAllister pushed his empty cup away. "Most of the lady archaeologists I've seen look as if somebody had dug them up by mistake and they should have been pushed back down in the hole again. Not like that luscious gal peering in the window, worse luck."

The lady tourist with the ankles and the trim figure settled a floppy-brimmed hat more firmly on her shoulder-length reddish-blonde hair and moved gracefully toward the other side of the square.

Jim watched her go with regret. "I wonder if she spoke English," he mused.

"Has the language barrier ever given you any trouble?"

The younger man flashed a sudden grin.

"Not that you'd notice. A little sign language adds zest to the chase."

"Are you ever serious?"

"You bet—when I'm back home after one of these reserve stints. Between a heavy court schedule and trying to keep the senior partners of the firm happy, there's not much time for anything else except some weekend sailing down in the Keys."

Thorson stared benevolently at Jim's broad shoulders, the sharp cheek bones accentuating his keen gaze, and the determined chin that boded ill in any dispute. "I don't imagine there's a struggle to get feminine crew on that boat of yours. . . ."

"Belay that," Jim said firmly. "You needn't make me sound like a bull calf larking around in the meadow. Since my sailboat's only a twenty-foot sloop, I can manage it nicely alone, thanks."

"I like to hear you using those nautical expressions." Thorson's tone was amiably wicked. "It keeps reminding me of your true place in all this."

"Adam, for two cents I'd twist your neck until I hear the real reason why I'm about to get on a rather small Italian passenger-freighter and do a milk run around the eastern Mediterranean. With only two more weeks of my reserve tour left, I hadn't planned anything more laborious than separating my paper clips from the rubber bands."

"Probably that's why the admiral decided you were just the man for this job." Adam raised a defensive hand as he saw Jim's sudden movement. "All right, all right. Simmer down, man—it shouldn't be all that bad. I can give you a little bit of the background. We'll let Miss Halliday fill in the final details aboard the ship after we sail. She's due to fly in from Paris today."

"Blast Miss Halliday. Get on with the explanation."

"Very well." Thorson took another sip of coffee and made a wry face as he swallowed it. "I can never get used to this stuff and when it's cold as well . . ."

"Stop changing the subject."

Adam shook his head sorrowfully before saying, "Actually the background on this came about two years ago. There wasn't much in the papers at the time partly because of a lack of public interest in archaeology and partly because museum thefts don't rate headlines for long. Possibly you remember that some jewelry was stolen from the London Museum's Egyptian collection while the pieces were on the continent for exhibit. These particular articles turned up missing after they had been shown in Paris, although the actual theft wasn't discovered until the pieces were being unpacked in Amsterdam. As I said, the publicity was held to a minimum. But I should add," and his lean face suddenly became grim, "that all the law enforcement agencies on the continent agreed to cooperate as soon as they heard exactly what was stolen."

A furrow creased McAllister's forehead. "I take it somebody really made off with the goodies."

"You could safely say that. At least I'd call two bracelets and a massive gold collar from the XIIth Egyptian Dynasty one of the better hauls."

Jim gave a soft, drawn-out whistle. "My lord, I had no idea. The value would be tremendous."

"Beyond price, of course. The collar has a human-headed hawk which is the symbol of the soul, with precious jewels inlaid on the outspread wings. Even the back is chased in magnificent feather work. The gold bracelets were made for a princess and show Harpocrates on a jewel-encrusted lotus leaf." Adam leaned forward to say earnestly, "But more than the intrinsic value, there's the prestige of ownership. Putting it bluntly, the British want them back. Period, full stop, and exclamation point! And aside from declaring war, they're overlooking no chances of recovery." He sat back again. "But it has to be kept quiet. With the Mideast in a turmoil now, they don't want to furnish another bone of contention to either side."

"But where do we come in?" Jim asked. "I lost all my connections with the archaeological set as soon as the secretary married a political science major with a bankroll."

"Just as well for you that she did," Thorson said unfeelingly. "As far as the trail of our missing merchandise goes, the museum authorities were especially suspicious of one of the men who was connected with the transport of the exhibits at the time of the loss. Ostensibly, he was working on the Egyptian collection for his doctoral thesis—when his research didn't interfere with wine, women, and all the rest."

"He doesn't sound like the typical archaeologist."

Adam nodded grimly. "Fortunately or unfortunately, there's papa's bankroll in the background, so he doesn't have to take his academic work too seriously. In the past, he's never let his studies get in the way of his drinking."

"That kind, eh. What's the name of this character?"

"Albert Rousch." Thorson's scholarly face lit with humor. "Believe it or not, he's the reason for your being here."

"Oh, I'll believe it. Is there more to the story or do I have to buy you another cup of coffee for that?"

"Decent of you, my boy, but I'll take a rain check."

"And you can skip that phony British accent too," Jim told him balefully. "If you go home talking like that, they'll throw you out of British Columbia."

"It's all part of my cover," the other said, grinning. "I thought I was getting the hang of it very well."

"In the field of espionage, you and I both come in the slow learner class. We couldn't convince anybody if we wore trenchcoats and drove an Aston-Martin. This must be a very low budget effort." He stared at the fabled bronze horses above the main portal of St. Mark's. "It seems sillier than ever when you're in a place like this."

"Those horses you're admiring were cast in Alexander the Great's time and survived being transferred from Constantinople during the Fourth Crusade. At least, transferred is the word used now," Thorson said simply. "Can you imagine this square without them or that fifteenth-century clock with the famous bronze Moors hammering out the hours?"

The younger man waited for him to go on.

"At the risk of sounding pontifical," Adam said, "the items we're looking for are just as important in the scheme of things."

"I refuse to get drawn into an argument on classicism." McAllister crossed his ankles and slouched down more comfortably in his chair. "Let's agree that the missing items from the Egyptian collection deserve top priority. That still doesn't stop me from feeling like a damn fool when I have to spend two weeks dogging some female archaeologist's footsteps."

"Blame Albert Rousch for that."

"Personally or in the general run of things?"

"Both, I suppose." Thorson's thinning gray hair blew into his eyes as a flock of pigeons swooped low and he ducked to avoid their flight. "I'm for the Audubon Society and all that," he said testily, "but it seems to me the citizens of Venice are in more danger from being taken over by the birds than they are by having their buildings sink into the sea."

"Very interesting commentary." Jim's broad grin flashed. "What about Mr. Rousch?"

"Don't rush me. As I said before he was working in a semi-official capacity for the museum when the items disappeared, and naturally he was questioned by the authorities at length. He couldn't prove that he didn't have anything to do with the thefts; on the other hand, they couldn't prove that he did. The result was a complete standoff. Rousch's dossier had enough irregularities in it to encourage the British C.I.D. to keep a weather eye on him since the robbery. Lately, the word got out that he was planning a junket to the Middle East. Since there's no actual evidence against him, they can't tell him to stay and play in the Roman ruins they're unearthing in England.

"So ... Mr. Rousch has secured passage on the *Lucarno*. Ostensibly, he's making the full cruise and debarking at Marseilles; the British believe he'll leave the ship in Syria or Lebanon. Then he'll pick up the treasure from the spot where it's been hidden by a confederate and head for Cairo. There's no doubt the Egyptians would like the jewelry back, and they're not particular how they get it."

"But why is the United States Navy in on it?"

Thorson smiled dryly. "Because Albert Rousch is a United States citizen."

McAllister groaned. "I might have known."

"He is a dubious blessing, but your country seems to be stuck with him. Both parents were U.S. citizens and his father was an oil company employee at the time Rousch was born in the Mideast. Albert had a dual citizenship until age twenty-one and then chose the U.S. He still speaks English with a decided accent, but strangely enough, whenever he gets drunk he loudly proclaims his American heritage to everybody within shouting distance."

"Further glorifying the American image," Jim said bitterly. "Why couldn't we just drop him overboard one night when he's soused?"

"I don't think you'd be convicted if it could be arranged," Thorson told him. "Provided, of course, you recover the stolen articles first. Until then, Mr. Rousch can neither be bruised nor scratched."

"It sure sounds like a frost of a cruise." McAllister rubbed the side of his nose reflectively. "I'm on tap because of the involvement of an American citizen and a long-forgotten archaeology course. Add a withered career woman and a stubborn Canadian . . ."

". . . who shall be nameless."

"Yeah. A nameless Canadian professor who's been spending his sabbatical sweeping out the cobwebs in the basement of the London Museum. I'll bet he was johnny-on-the-spot to volunteer."

"Naturally." Thorson's thin lips quirked upward. "It was dark in that basement and he wanted out."

"By the way, weren't you in some hush-hush thing during the war?"

"Forget about that. Hopefully, I'm along to identify the jewelry and hold your hand."

"Well, that's a switch. I was afraid all the hand-holding activities were between me and Madame Elisaveta."

"You're being too hasty, Jim. She might turn out to be a charming young lady."

"With a background like hers? On the shady side of twenty-four, unmarried, and more academic degrees than a mail-order physician." The younger man shook his head. "She sounds completely zilch."

Thorson pointed his pipe stem at him. "You just celebrated your thirtieth birthday and you're not scheduled for the next trip to the tomb."

"It's different with a woman. For one thing, she's an administrator with the Smith–Forbes Foundation. I'll let Miss Halliday collect a donation from me for the cause any time because they've financed a lot of digs around the world and deserve all the recognition they can get. As far as collecting anything more personal—no thanks. Just deal me out—preferably with a trendy doll who has trouble looking up numbers in the telephone directory."

"I think you're making a mistake."

"Don't you believe it. Did she volunteer for this jaunt?"

Thorson shrugged. "I don't know. The only thing I heard was that she might be a stabilizing influence on Rousch."

"You mean she can stand on deck murmuring statistics on the Egyptian collection into his ear when there's a moon?" Jim snorted and made motions to the hovering waiter for their check. "Those bosses of yours better stop reading espionage novels and see how the world is run. Frankly, I don't expect to get anything out of this two weeks except a case of sunburn and a dose of boredom." He looked at the tab on the check and reached in his pocket for some coins. "At least, I can look forward to getting back home at the end of it. That Florida landscape is going to look mighty good." He sighed reminiscently. "Blue sky, sunshine, sailing off the Keys . . . man, that's the life for me."

Thorson tapped out his pipe on the heel of his shoe. "I wouldn't call Naples 'hardship duty.' "

"That's for sure," McAllister left a tip by his saucer, "although there's getting to be so much smog there that it's almost as bad as parts of

Los Angeles. Maybe we'll get some real fresh air in Syria and Lebanon." He shoved back his metal chair and got up. "That is, if we're not in the fog of intrigue all the time."

Thorson put his pipe carefully back in his jacket pocket. "Maybe the museum people thought Miss Halliday could clear away the mists. At any rate, she can bring us up to date when we get aboard ship. Do you want to head for the *vaporetto* pier?"

Jim looked at his watch. "We don't have to board the *Lucarno* until six, so there's no point in taking an early water bus. Let's spend an hour or so looking for some Murano glass. It's time I sent some presents home."

"Keeping up the social amenities?"

"Something like that. It never hurts to renew your lines of communication."

"That's the trouble with you Americans," Adam said sorrowfully, falling into step beside him. "Thinking, always thinking."

"Who can do any rational thinking in Venice?" Jim complained mildly. "It's a good thing we're leaving today or I'd probably be out pricing a palazzo on the Grand Canal. There's something about this place. . . ."

"Casanova would have agreed with you," Thorson said, strolling along but taking a last look over his shoulder at the Gothic arches of the Doge's Palace, "so would Lord Byron who fell in love here, Canaletto who painted here, or Browning who died here. You're in illustrious company."

Jim stuck his hands in his trouser pockets and turned down one of the narrow streets. "I wonder if our Elisaveta ever warms her soul to the magic of a place like this?" He kicked idly at a piece of debris near the bottom of a stone bridge arching a canal. "Probably not. I can see her now, checking her luggage to see if her hot water bottle is handy and she has plenty of aspirin."

"You're being pessimistic," Adam said gloomily, "but there's a chance you're right."

Actually, they were completely wrong. The object of their speculation was, at that moment, in a modest shop not far from them. It was a store specializing in women's apparel and English-speaking clerks.

Elisaveta Halliday was holding up a drab gray knitted dress in front of her and looking at it speculatively. "I think this one might do," she said finally to the saleswoman beside her. "It looks as if the skirt's long enough."

"But signorina . . ." The clerk was torn between her innate sense of honesty and the desire to make a sale. Finally, she succumbed to the former. "It does nothing for the skin or your beautiful hair." She cast an admiring glance at the gleaming strawberry blonde mane curling gently on her client's shoulders.

Lisa Halliday looked again at the plain round collar of the dress, the straight bodice attached to the severe skirt. There was no doubt about it; it was just the thing for mopping a kitchen floor or clearing a bird's nest out of the chimney. Her eyes narrowed in sudden decision. "I'll take it," she announced, thrusting it at the deflated saleswoman. "Can you wrap it for me while I look for a pair of shoes at the shop over there?" She pointed across the narrow street.

"Of course, signorina," the clerk's countenance brightened immediately. "Some shoes would do much to brighten the color. They have a new style in the window," she bubbled happily, "I saw them when I came to work this morning. A marvelous sandal in gray and yellow leather with a high, tapering heel. Beautiful with anything—even this dress," she added with forced honesty.

"I'm sure you're right," Lisa said, pausing at the door, "but I had something else in mind. Black . . . low heels . . . and a really good arch support. . . . It's necessary for my work," she explained somewhat grimly, "my colleagues expect it of me."

"I see, signorina." The saleswoman nodded in a resigned fashion. "Probably the shop will have something of that type. Your package will be ready when you return."

"*Grazie.*" Lisa smiled and closed the shop door behind her.

The clerk watched her go into the shoe salon and then come out a minute or so later with a salesman behind her to point at a pair of shoes in the back of the window display. They were black, low-heeled, eminently sensible, and undoubtedly had a splendid arch support.

The woman in the dress shop shook her head ruefully and looked down at the dreary knitted dress in her hand. Americans! She shook her head again. They were absolutely beyond comprehension. Such an attractive young lady, too. Fortunately, Venetian men felt differently about things. She looked complacently down at her clinging skirt, which showed a generous expanse of knee and thigh.

Even if they had gotten to the moon first, there was no doubt about it. The American men were crazy!

CHAPTER TWO

The M.S. *Lucarno* was riding low in the water at her pier when Jim and Adam came alongside later that afternoon. On the dock, workmen were loading pallets aboard forklifts, while aboard ship, hatch covers were being secured both fore and aft. Crewmen who had been supervising the loading stood talking desultorily at the rail, looking grimy and hot in cotton undershirts and dark blue work pants. Their appearance obviously didn't trouble them, however, as they smoked and pushed their old-fashioned sailor hats back still further on their heads.

"The ship looks in pretty good shape," Jim said, glancing at the white hull. "If they've loaded the cargo properly we should have a smooth trip, even if the displacement is quite a bit below what we might call normal."

"Mmmm." Adam's look was more dubious. "I'm just as glad we're only cruising the Med. Frankly, I can't imagine crossing the Atlantic in a peapod like this."

"So speaks today's traveler." Jim shook his head. "You're used to 747's—a stewardess to bring you roast beef and a new movie on the wide screen." He nodded toward the short, steep gangway. "Don't be put off by the lack of amenities. Italians usually run a darned good ship."

Adam moved ahead of him and grinned back over his shoulder as he stepped onto the wooden platform. "Look who's defending the *Lucarno!* I thought you were the one having a fit about all this."

"Not the ship. Just the passengers." Jim's foot slipped slightly on the first step and he clutched the heavy parcel he was carrying more tightly. "Damn! This thing weighs a ton."

Adam paused halfway up. "Want some help?"

The other shook his head. "No thanks, besides, you're a little late with the offer. Why didn't you stop me before I paid out the cold cash?"

Thorson stepped on deck and waited for him to catch up. "I did suggest that you have the package shipped," he reminded his friend, "and you gave me a five-minute lecture on how it would be broken before it ever arrived in the States."

"Did anyone ever tell you that logic is the least appreciated virtue?" Jim stepped off the gangway and shifted the parcel to his other arm. "I feel as if I'd been carrying a baby elephant for the past two hours." He flexed his left hand gingerly. "Lead on, before I'm tempted to drop the damn thing overboard."

Adam held open the swinging door leading into a main deck corridor. "Not now that the end is finally in sight—there's the purser's hangout down behind that counter. We'd better report in and see if our luggage is aboard."

A chunky, prematurely gray-haired man in a starched, white uniform greeted them. *"Buona sera—"* he hesitated and then went on, "or should I say good evening? It is Dr. Thorson and Mr. McAllister, isn't it?"

"That's right," Jim said putting his parcel down on the office counter with a sigh of relief. "I'm McAllister."

The purser stuck out a cordial hand. "And I'm Leonardo Vanni. Call me Leon."

Thorson shook hands looking puzzled. "You don't sound any more Italian than I do."

"That's not surprising. I was born in Italy but I went to live with an uncle in the Bronx when I was going to school." He shrugged elaborately. "My knowledge of English comes in handy for this job, and maybe it'll get me a place on one of the company's trans-Atlantic liners eventually."

"I see. Well, it will be a relief to put away my Italian phrase book for the next two weeks," Thorson assured him.

Leon made an expansive gesture. "You won't have any trouble aboard the *Lucarno*. Most of the crew understand at least a couple of languages and we'll make sure you get a dining room waiter who specializes in English. The bartender isn't very fluent, but his martinis don't lose anything in the translation."

He peered down at the typewritten list on the counter and then reached into a glass-fronted cabinet and put down two keys in front of them. "You have adjoining staterooms. Dr. Thorson, yours is number seven and Mr. McAllister has number nine. The steward is still working on them but they should be ready in about half an hour."

"There's no rush," Jim said, dropping his key in his jacket pocket. "Do you know if our luggage got aboard all right?"

Leon nodded reassuringly. "Just a few minutes ago. Roberto—that's your steward—took it down. If you'd like to go up and have a drink in the lounge," he glanced at his watch, "your cabins will be ready well before dinner. We'll be serving at seven thirty tonight—right after we sail."

"Sounds fine." Jim gave his package a sour look before hoisting it again in his arms.

"I can get Roberto to take that down to your cabin for you, Mr. McAllister."

Jim hesitated perceptibly, tempted by the offer, then shook his head. "No thanks. The darned thing's become an obsession with me by now. I'm going to get this piece of glass home in one piece or know the reason why."

Leon's smile became suddenly understanding. "Ah, I understand. You've been buying Murano glass. You aren't the first passenger to come aboard carrying such a parcel."

"No, and I'm sure I won't be the last. I only hope that the other poor devils don't choose a camel that weighs as much as a dinosaur." He clutched the package tighter. "I need a drink after this safari. Let's go, Adam."

"I'm right with you. Oh, by the way," Thorson paused and turned back to the counter, "has Miss Halliday come aboard yet, Leon?"

The purser surveyed his list and then shook his head. "Not yet, but there are several passengers still due to arrive."

"I see, thanks. See you later, then." Thorson gave him a thoughtful nod and followed Jim down the corridor toward the curving stairway amidships.

Up one deck, they found themselves in a central foyer opening onto the public rooms. They glanced into a deserted dining salon furnished with a cluster of tables, the starched white tablecloths and gleaming cutlery looking a trifle incongruous aboard the small freighter. The dining area was flanked by an equally deserted combination cardroom and library. Two bridge tables were placed forlornly in the center of it, and on one wall, bookshelves showed a multilingual collection of paperbacks donated by previous passengers.

"*War and Peace* side by side with *The Five Little Peppers and How They Grew,*" said Jim

28

who had walked over to peruse the titles. "Or if you'd rather, there's *Principles of Socialism,* vol. 3, in German." He shook his head regretfully. "Talk about mixed bags!"

"It looks as if you were right about the catering, at least," Thorson acknowledged. "The dining room is mighty attractive—they've even got fresh carnations on the tables."

Jim nodded. "Food's one thing the Italians never take for granted. We'll probably gain twenty pounds on the pasta during this trip but what a way to go!"

They re-entered the foyer and pushed open heavy glass doors into a spacious lounge with wide windows overlooking the forward cargo deck. Magazines covered the top of a grand piano, which was pushed into one corner of the room; upholstered chairs edged the pocket-sized dance floor in the center. A good-sized bar with a gleaming chrome espresso machine atop it was recessed in another corner of the room. Behind the bar counter, a white-jacketed bartender was busily polishing glasses. He looked up and nodded as the two men slid onto leather-topped bar stools.

"Buona sera."

"Good evening," Adam responded and turned to Jim, who was easing his parcel down on the counter. "What are you going to have now that the sun is over the yardarm or wherever it's supposed to go?"

McAllister raised his eyebrows. "Since when

has the time of day affected your drinking habits?"

"It doesn't, that was merely for your benefit," Adam said austerely. "I'm having scotch and soda," he told the bartender.

"And I'll start with a long glass of iced tonic water. Carrying this damned camel has made me as parched as one," Jim complained.

"Tonic water—no gin?" The bartender looked puzzled.

"That's right. Plain tonic water."

The man hesitated and then shrugged elaborately. *"Si, signore."* His resigned look showed that the passenger must be humored.

"I'd like another look at that purchase of yours," Adam said.

"So would I," Jim admitted with a sheepish grin. "I bought it a little faster than usual; I think I got carried away." He glanced over at Adam's pained expression. "That was not intended as a pun."

"I sincerely hope not."

James unknotted the string on the bulky parcel and thrust it in his pocket before peeling the paper back and carefully lifting out a chunky glass camel. Set on a modernistic base, the clear crystal of the body blended softly into a gold and then a burnt-orange shade for the center core. The long neck arched gracefully away from the main piece and a slender head stared at them disdainfully.

"He looks as if he might spit in your eye at

any minute," Adam said, considering it carefully, "but it's a magnificent piece of design. I think he'll be worth the excess luggage charge to get him home."

Jim surveyed his purchase through narrowed eyes and then grinned suddenly. "I agree. He's an objet d'art with personality."

The bartender was beaming now. It was obvious that the American appreciated Venetian glass even though he had strange drinking habits. As he set the glasses in front of Adam and Jim, the bartender's look suddenly extended to a point just beyond their shoulders. "Would the signorina like something as well?"

"Signorina?" Jim repeated blankly.

Adam's reaction was even more studied. He pushed his glass back carefully and turned slowly on the bar stool. "Ah—" he said hesitantly, getting to his feet, "I'm Adam Thorson and you must be. . . ."

"I'm Elisaveta Halliday. How do you do," came a crisp voice from behind Jim's right shoulder.

He swiveled his bar stool around and let his glance start at the floor. The first six inches did little to encourage him.

Two sensible black shoes complete with neat ties and sturdy low heels stood in an uncompromising straight line three feet away. Ankles were hidden in gray lisle stockings thick enough to wear forever, and knees were nonexistent under the hem of a straight knitted skirt.

Jim blinked once, tightened his lips, and went up with the survey. If there was a waistline, it was shrouded under a thick belt. Above it, the unadorned bodice hung in sacklike folds down from a severe collar.

Elisaveta Halliday stared defiantly back at him when he got to chin level. There was probably nothing wrong with her chin except that it looked just as determined as his. A nice pair of lips compressed into a decisive line were unadorned, so she undoubtedly scorned make-up as well. Her watchful deep blue eyes were shaded by severe, black-framed sun glasses which had a tendency to slip down a haughty nose. As he completed his deliberate fact-finding tour, her hands came up nervously to poke back untidy strands of mouse-colored hair into an old-fashioned bun on the nape of her neck.

James sighed audibly and pushed his glass back toward the bartender. "You'd better put in some gin—quite a slug of it," he said before slowly getting to his feet.

The bartender's nod was understanding.

"And this is James McAllister," Adam was saying hurriedly, "on reserve duty with your navy."

Miss Halliday nodded distantly. "I've heard of Lieutenant McAllister." The inference in the pool of silence that followed made Jim feel that his next service promotion would be slow in coming if she had anything to do with it.

Adam was struggling hard with the social

amenities. "You'll join us, of course, Miss Halliday."

"Thank you," she inclined her head the slightest margin.

"Then let's adjourn to these chairs." Thorson gestured toward the center of the lounge. "They look a good deal more comfortable."

"Go ahead," Jim told him. "I'll be right with you." He picked up his camel and clutched it securely before reaching for his drink with the other hand.

"It's all right, signore," the bartender forestalled him by putting down a small tray. "I bring the drinks to you. Do you know what the lady will want?"

"I could make an educated guess—"

"Signore?"

Jim shook his head. "Never mind—you'd better ask." He strolled over to the chairs where Adam and Miss Halliday were settling and pulled up another alongside. The camel was placed carefully on a coffee table at his elbow.

Miss Halliday watched with lifted eyebrows. "What a remarkable animal," she said finally. "Do you take it with you everywhere?"

"Practically," James said, giving her a glance through narrowed eyes. The velvety tones underlying her speaking voice were oddly at variance with that spinster appearance. He continued blandly, "In a way, it's become a kind of security symbol. I had to leave my night light at home."

Adam swallowed the wrong way and came close to strangling in the process. "I'm afraid Jim is pulling your leg, Miss Halliday," he said in choked tones.

"No need to become offensive, Adam," James tut-tutted.

Miss Halliday's lips thinned even more drastically.

The bartender arrived providentially with their two drinks and a small saucer of potato chips which he placed on the table in front of them. "The signorina would like something?" he asked tentatively.

Elisaveta thought for a moment. "Possibly something nonalcoholic." She turned to Adam. "What would you recommend?"

"Well, there's tonic water or lemonade."

"Lemonade." She nodded decisively. "The very thing."

"Limonata for the signorina," the bartender repeated as he walked off, shaking his head.

James's camel seemed to possess a fascination for Miss Halliday and she leaned forward to stroke it gently while they were waiting for the arrival of her drink. "Quite an unusual design," she murmured, turning the statuette carefully with slender, rose-tipped fingers.

So Eliza-baby had her moments of vanity, after all, James thought, noting the nail polish.

"It's strange you should choose a camel," she

was saying. "From what I've heard they bray and spit . . ."

"And generally smell bad," he finished for her. "Their personal habits don't matter unless you collect live ones. So far, I haven't been tempted."

"I don't think there are many camels for sale where we're going," she countered, "so Dr. Thorson and I will try to keep you from temptation."

Jim's grin was full of devilment. "You can try, Miss Halliday, you can certainly try."

"Limonata for the signorina." The drink was placed in front of her by a white-jacketed waiter this time.

"Thank you." She lifted her glass. "What do you call your camel, Mr. McAllister?"

"What do you mean, call him?"

"His name. Surely he has a name?"

"Not yet. What do you suggest?"

Elisaveta bit her lip thoughtfully. "How about Shadrach?"

"Shadrach?" Jim considered it. "From out of the flames, you mean?" He smiled, this time without malice. "Very good, Miss Halliday. Shadrach it is."

"All right then, let's drink to Operation Shadrach." She took a sip of her lemonade, wrinkled her nose at its tartness, and then put the glass back on the table. "If we're going to be sent out here for a cops and robbers chase, we'd better get in character."

"Precisely what I've been telling Jim." Adam leaned back in his chair and fumbled for his pipe. "Do you mind if I smoke?"

"Not at all." She anchored her glasses more firmly on the bridge of her nose. "Perhaps we should go over what's to be accomplished on this trip since we aren't in danger of being overheard at the moment."

"There are two passengers just coming through the door," said Jim, who was facing that way, "but I don't know who they are. He's a short, pugnacious geezer with a swarthy complexion and she's a blonde dish considerably younger than he is. Maybe that is one of those Mideastern intrigues they're always talking about."

Elisaveta directed a squelching glance at him before turning and nodding to the couple who had paused by the bar. "That's Max Altose and his wife," she said settling back. "I just met them down at the purser's office. No mystery there."

"Sorry, Miss Halliday." Jim pulled at an imaginary forelock. "That blonde doesn't look like the rose-covered cottage type to me. Especially if Altose goes with the cottage."

"Possibly you're wrong just this once. Not all men have to be six feet tall and on the . . . er . . . rugged side to be attractive to the opposite sex."

"You'd know better than I," he said, unperturbed. "What does this Altose do, besides

36

being a source of continual enjoyment to his mate?"

She flushed under his sardonic gaze. "According to the information I received, he's a retired businessman from New York who has archaeology for a hobby. This is his first trip to Syria and Lebanon."

"How about Mrs. Altose?"

"I don't know."

Jim looked over toward the couple who were now huddled deep in conversation. "I wonder if they're a pair of newlyweds? That setup is a little too good to be true."

"Oh really!" From anyone else it would have been a snort of exasperation.

He waggled an admonitory finger. "Wait and see, Miss Halliday. Adam will tell you that I have an infallible instinct when it comes to the fair sex."

Thorson broke in, "In that case, Jim, what about the new arrival—that gray-haired woman chatting with the purser?"

"Ask Miss Halliday, she's evidently covered the field." James put his glass on the table beside Shadrach and reached for a cigarette. "Do you smoke?" he asked her.

"Very seldom," she replied stiffly, "so no thank you. The woman you're talking about is Carla Broome. We met earlier today at the steamship office. She's an American citizen who writes for one of the women's magazines, but she's currently on a holiday."

"Another innocuous tourist." He was patently amused. "It's amazing how many Americans have suddenly decided that this Italian puddle-jumper is the last word in touring. Miss Broome looks more like the Grenoble type, or Corfu, at the least. What do you think, Adam?"

Thorson puffed reflectively at his pipe, letting the smoke wreath his interested gaze. "S'hard to tell. That gray hair is deceiving. She's not more than forty. Damned good figure, too."

Elisaveta choked on her lemonade. "Really, Dr. Thorson. I didn't expect a remark like that from you."

"Why ever not. Just because I'm a professor doesn't mean I'm completely dead, my dear. I think the lady in question is coming this way. Perhaps you'd be good enough to perform the introductions."

"Good evening, Miss Halliday." Carla Broome's voice was brisk but pleasant. "I'm sorry to make your gentlemen struggle to their feet," her warm, dark-eyed gaze roved appreciatively over McAllister's tall figure and then lingered longer on Thorson's spare one, "but it looks as if this is one of those trips where we'll all be gathering in ethnic groups." A charming smile flickered. "I'm Carla Broome and quite frankly I'm delighted to discover such presentable specimens of American manhood aboard."

"Do Canadians count too?" Adam asked hopefully. On seeing her smile widen he added, "It works both ways, Miss Broome. We had no idea things would be so pleasant on the distaff side. I'm Adam Thorson and this is Jim McAllister. Apparently you've already met Miss Halliday."

"Yes, she helped me out at the ticket counter when I was getting bogged down in a welter of Italian red tape. How are you, Miss Halliday?" Carla's tone was quizzical as she glanced down at the other's bowed head. "I scarcely recognized you."

"I'm very well, thank you," the younger woman said faintly. "Won't you join us?"

"I can't, thanks. The purser has promised to help me out on my currency problems. Somehow, I've collected too many French francs and I must get them switched into lire before we get into Turkish money or Lebanese—whatever do they use in Lebanon?"

"It's a Lebanese pound," Jim told her. "About 3.21 to an American dollar. If you're in any doubt, they're happy to take an American greenback."

"Most people are." Carla smiled again. "It was nice to see you, but I'd better scoot and get my finances untangled before the dinner gong." She gave them a brief wave and disappeared out into the foyer.

"Seems nice," Jim said, sitting down again. "Things are improving, Adam."

Elisaveta cleared her throat irritably. "I

thought we were discussing the reason for our being here, Mr. McAllister."

"By all means. Do continue," he said stiffly.

"Very well. According to my information, two other passengers to come aboard at this part of the trip are a Frau Witten and her twelve-year-old son. They're from West Germany and she's some sort of teacher. Mrs. Witten speaks only German, so probably our paths won't cross too frequently." She hesitated and then went on. "That brings us up to Mr. Rousch."

"Which rhymes with ouch," offered James, "either coincidentally or on purpose."

"Mr. Rousch," she continued, "is to be under our constant surveillance during the voyage."

"For lord's sake, do we tuck him in at night, too? This gets worse all the time."

"Surveillance within reason. The authorities are reasonably sure that Mr. Rousch does not have the items on board, although we're supposed to go through his things if we can."

"Simplicity itself," Jim said. "All you have to do is sit up here drinking with him while Adam and I go through his cabin." His look flickered over her. "You'd better recruit Carla to help you."

Injured feminine pride came to the forefront. "Don't you think I could keep Mr. Rousch up here by myself?"

"Maybe you could." The tone left her smarting by its very insouciance. "It takes all kinds, after all."

Adam waded in before the situation worsened. "I gather that the jewelry is supposed to have been smuggled to the Near East before this."

Miss Halliday allowed herself to be diverted. "The latest is that Mr. Rousch has booked air passage to Cairo from Beirut two days after the *Lucarno*'s arrival there, so he must be planning a pickup of the treasure." She peered at Thorson, looking like a solemn owl in the process. "It's a double booking; he still has his ship ticket to Marseilles."

Adam whistled softly. "What does it sound like to you, Jim?"

"Like the delivery date or payoff couldn't be made earlier than Beirut."

The other nodded. "Two days gives him plenty of opportunities to make all the contacts he wants."

Elisaveta shook her head. "He won't have much time for that."

"Why not?" Jim asked.

"Because he's signed up for two days of shore tours. One afternoon, he's scheduled for the crusaders' castle at Byblos. The next day, there's a tour to see the Roman ruins at Baalbek. Perhaps he has plans of his own for the rest of the time."

Jim scratched the top of his nose absently,

then he shook his head slowly but definitely. "I don't get it."

Thorson gave him a questioning glance.

"It doesn't make sense," McAllister said. "If Rousch is preparing to fly off with a bagful of expensive knickknacks, why is he spending his time sightseeing like an Ohio schoolteacher? It makes about as much sense as making a Christmas Club deposit the day before you rob the bank."

"Not necessarily," Adam argued. "If the delivery is to be made at the last minute, Rousch is making sure that he doesn't attract undue attention. It would look conspicuous if he didn't go on a shore excursion; he'd be as out-of-place on a cruise ship as a tourist without a camera."

"Umm—you may be right, but it sounds too pat for my money. What do you want to bet that Mr. Rousch has the laugh on us?"

"There's no need for you to be so pessimistic about it, Mr. McAllister," Elisaveta put in.

"A lawyer's always pessimistic about things, Miss Halliday." He paused to give her an irritable look and went on, "Miss Halliday's an awful mouthful if we're going to be together for two weeks. How about substituting something shorter?"

Her look through the severe spectacles was enigmatic. "There's always 'Hey you'," she suggested.

"There is, but for the sake of the cause my

name is Jim and that's Adam," he nodded toward Thorson who was hiding a grin. "So—"

She sat up straighter on the chair. "As you know, my given name is Elisaveta."

"Then you must have encountered this problem before. What does it shorten to—Eliza or what?"

"My friends call me Lisa." She emphasized the second word.

"That's strange." He stared at her. "I could have sworn you were more the type for. . . ."

"Or perhaps you object to that, too."

"Not at all, my dear," Adam put in nimbly. "Lisa's a charming name. I meant to ask if this assignment interfered with your other plans?"

She shook her head, the flush still in her cheeks from McAllister's scarcely flattering inference. "Not really. I was attending a conference in Paris so it merely meant postponing my return home for two weeks."

"And where is home?" he pursued gently.

"San Diego. The foundation's main office is in New York, but for the last year or so they've maintained a West Coast headquarters. Naturally, I was delighted because that meant I had a chance to get back home."

"So you're from California originally?"

She nodded enthusiastically. "Southern California, Los Angeles really."

There was a disdainful snort from Jim as he leaned forward to select a potato chip.

"Do you disapprove of that too, Mr. McAllister?" Her tone took on icicles again.

"Jim," he corrected automatically, and brushed the salt from his fingers.

"Is there something wrong with southern California?"

"I've always thought so," he told her. "My home is in Miami."

"Oh . . . Florida." She sounded as if an insect had just been sighted in the salad. "I've been in Florida twice," she said sweetly. "Once was in December during an 'unseasonable' cold spell. The only heater in the motel was an air conditioner run backward. It was so cold in my room that I ran the hot water in the bathroom taps just to try and get warm."

"Now look here. . . ."

"The other time was in the summer," she went on relentlessly. "I was down in the Keys that time. I remember the place well; it is the only time in my life that I have shared a telephone booth with six mosquitos. I counted them on my ankle while I was waiting for the operator to put a call through."

"See here, Miss Halliday . . ." his tone was incensed.

"Lisa, please," she purred.

He ignored that. "Thousands of visitors come to Florida each year," he said hotly, "so we won't miss your patronage. And if you want to go on in this line, I could mention a nasty California word called smog."

"Please don't," Adam said firmly. "At the moment, we're leaving Venice, which certainly should be neutral ground." He shook his head at both of them. "No wonder you Americans have trouble with your domestic affairs. I thought the California–Florida feud went out with Calvin Coolidge." He rattled the ice in his glass suggestively. "I'm ready for another drink. What about some more lemonade, Lisa?"

Her hand trembled slightly as she reached for a potato chip. "No thank you, Adam."

"Jim, can you get that bartender's attention? Our waiter has disappeared."

McAllister obligingly turned in his chair and then remained frozen in that position. "My God!" he said in a flat tone of voice. "Look what's just come in."

As if directed by a puppeteer, Lisa and Adam swiveled to stare at the newest arrival.

The object of their concern paused on the edge of the dance floor and surveyed the room impartially. He was a short, thick man in his early thirties; his fair hair cut so close that it resembled an untidy patch of stubble. The stubble continued down over reddened cheeks and a chin that he had neglected to shave recently. He was dressed in a striped blue and white T-shirt and wrinkled blue jeans, with his sockless feet stuck in sloppy loafers. In one hand, he clutched a red felt alpine hat with a high crown and narrow brim. He stared at the room's occupants as he stood there, swaying far more than any movement of the ship required. Then he seemed to focus on Lisa's quiet figure and he lurched toward her.

"Fair lady," he swept the ridiculous hat down in an Elizabethan type bow, almost falling onto the table in front of her in the process.

There was a rumble of displeasure at her side as James hitched his chair forward to protect both her and his glass camel. Neither he nor Adam made any pretense of standing to acknowledge the man's presence.

"Fair lady," the man said again, managing to stand erect with difficulty. "Since we're going to be passengers together, I thought I should come over and introduce myself. Rousch is my name—Albert Rousch." His words were barely discernible due to a thick accent and the heavy load of alcohol.

"Why don't you come back another time," Jim said levelly. "We'll be around."

Thick lips curved in a vacant smile as Rousch shifted his feet to turn and look at McAllister rather than merely moving his head. "Be 'round," the man repeated, pleased with the sound of the words. "We'll all be 'round." He peered down at them again. "You're speakin' English," he said accusingly.

"Go to the head of the class," Jim told him patiently. "I think the purser is looking for you."

"'Mericans, huh?" The vacant smile came again. "That's a coin-co-in—." Between the word and the liquor, he had to retrench. He swayed and brought his hat up to his chest as he wrestled mentally. Lisa's downbent head seemed to fascinate him in the interval. "Amazing," he finally managed triumphantly.

Jim succeeded in getting the attention of the waiter who had just re-entered the lounge. A curt nod of his head toward the drunken man made the crew man blink once and then move forward understandingly.

"Riully amazin'," the drunk continued as if there had been no pause. He raised his voice. "I'm a 'Merican too, whaddya think of that?"

"Not much," Jim said cheerfully. "We've learned to take all kinds of disasters in stride. Here's a man who's looking for you."

The waiter took a firm grip on the other's arm. "If you'll come this way, Signor Rousch. . . ."

The man allowed himself to be led unsteadily away, as if suddenly oblivious to the trio behind him.

"The waiter'd better hurry," Adam said thoughtfully, watching the two carefully negotiate the double doors. "It looks as if Rousch is about to pass out."

"So that's Albert Rousch," Lisa's tone was quiet—too quiet.

"The one and only," Jim said, not without sympathy. "Hey, don't look like that. Adam and I don't expect you to sacrifice your virtue even for a XIIth Dynasty necklace." He settled back in his chair. "Adam, the bartender's back in business, will you order another round. Sure you won't have something else, Lisa?"

She swallowed once and put out an unsteady hand to stroke Shadrach's smooth back, her mind obviously on the man who had just left. "Yes," she said, "I think I will. Whatever you're drinking." She nodded toward his glass and then looked up at Thorson. "Would you tell the man to put in some gin—as James said, quite a slug of it."

Adam nodded and went over to make their wants known.

McAllister rose from his chair and peered casually through the lounge window. "We should be paying attention to the scenery outside instead of the flotsam aboard. Darned if we're not having a slow tour down the Grand Canal. I think that's San Giorgio Maggiore coming up."

Adam returned and stood beside him. "You're right. It's fortunate we're sailing early enough to still get some view." He glanced down at Lisa with a sympathetic smile. "At least, it helps take the bad taste of Mr. Rousch out of our minds. He was the last of the boarding passengers until Brindisi, I think."

"In that case, something's off schedule," said Jim. "Look what's just floated in. He's a carbon copy of one of the muscle man candidates from a southern California surfing beach."

Lisa glanced over her shoulder and then gave

a half-gasp that earned a suspicious glance from McAllister.

"Don't tell me you know those padded shoulders," he said disparagingly.

"As a matter of fact, I do, and they're not padded."

"All right, I'll bite. Who is he—Clark Kent to the rescue?"

"Superman didn't work the Mediterranean," she said dryly. "This man is Alessandro Ceranini, an Italian who works in Beirut."

"Well, gird yourself for a happy reunion," he said in an undertone. "Lochinvar's headed this way."

"*Buona sera*, madame—gentlemen. The purser told me that I might introduce myself as we are fellow passengers to Beirut," the newcomer said in excellent English. "My name is Ceranini."

"I'm McAllister." Jim shook hands reluctantly. "And this is Dr. Adam Thorson. Of course you know Miss Halliday." His duty done, Jim turned to signal a waiter for another chair and thus missed the look of astonishment that came over Signor Ceranini's handsome face.

No one, however, could have missed the European's sudden explosion of laughter as he roared "Lisa—Lisa Halliday! I would not have recognized you in such clothes. Surely they're not having a fancy dress ball the first night out?"

There was no doubt that Lisa would have liked to disappear through the floor. Since that wasn't possible, she determined to brazen it out. "Don't be silly," she snapped. She defiantly met McAllister's puzzled look. "Sandro and I met in Los Angeles last winter when he was attending some meetings there," she explained. "He runs the Beirut bureau for a big Italian travel firm."

"As you would say, I am 'our man in Beirut,'" Ceranini said, beaming. He turned his benign expression on Lisa. "Very convenient to show you all the sights—when you get out of that ridiculous costume, of course. You look as if you are pretending to be somebody's mother-in-law."

The quiet atmosphere penetrated even his ebullient spirit then.

"What is wrong?" he demanded. "Did I drop a block?"

"Brick, Sandro," Lisa corrected automatically.

"Not at all," Thorson cut in. "Won't you have a drink with us, Signor Ceranini?"

"*Grazie.*"

"Perhaps you'd send my drink down to my cabin," Lisa appealed to Adam hurriedly, avoiding Jim McAllister's glower. "I would like to change for dinner."

"Of course, my dear."

"I'll see you later, Sandro," Lisa told him.

"It's lovely to have you aboard. We'll get together for a long chat."

"We must manage one of those too, Miss Halliday," Jim spoke up deliberately. "Perhaps later on at dinner. If you should have any trouble recognizing us, I'll be wearing a black necktie and Adam usually shows up in navy blue." A muscle flexed in his tight jaw as he looked her up and down once again. "If we're going to play more games, perhaps you'd give us a high sign so we'll be sure to know you."

Lisa clenched her teeth to avoid a hot reply, even though she realized his anger was justified. "Don't worry, Mr. McAllister," she purred as she turned to leave, "I'd recognize you anywhere but I'll have a rose in my teeth if I can find one."

"That won't be necessary," his tone was equally silky, "but any little thing would help, wouldn't it?"

CHAPTER THREE

Lisa was still seething from James McAllister's final remark when she reached the lower deck and started searching for the number of her stateroom.

There was an open door amidships and Carla Broome stuck her head out as Lisa went by.

"Hi neighbor!" The older woman leaned against the bulkhead and gave her a friendly smile. "Your cabin's next door. Can you come in and chat for a while?"

"I don't think I'd better," Lisa's voice was uneven. "I'm in for a major overhaul and I'd better get started. Come be my guest instead."

Carla consulted her watch. "All right, thanks. We still have a few minutes before the dinner gong."

Lisa moved on to the next stateroom door. "Number eight—I guess this is it."

"That's right—even numbers in this corridor, odd on the other side of the ship." Carla watched her push open the door and stand just inside to survey the room. "The cabins aren't bad."

"Not bad at all." Lisa walked over to inspect

the drawers of the dressing table. "Two good-sized portholes too," she said, moving over to flick aside the curtains.

"And the bed is comfortable," Carla added, settling down on the foot of it comfortably. "I can vouch for that."

Lisa had opened a door in the entrance-way. "Whee—a bathroom complete with tub. This is luxury!"

"We're among the favored ones on that score. Just the four cabins amidship have them."

Lisa was pulling combs out of her hair allowing it to fall back down to shoulder level. "I'm going to make use of those facilities and see if I can get my hair looking decent." She gave the mousy locks a dissatisfied yank.

"Hallelujah!" Carla leaned back comfortably on an elbow. "I don't know what you used to get that drab, streaked appearance but I couldn't believe you were the same person I'd met earlier today."

"That was the general idea," Lisa said a trifle ironically.

"Well, I liked the other one better. How you could do that to such gorgeous hair? Women spend their lives at the hairdressers trying to come out with your shade of reddish gold and you try to hide it."

"It was only a top dressing of powder." Lisa was pawing through her smaller suitcase as she spoke and finally pulled out a hairbrush with an exclamation of triumph.

"Are you going to volunteer the reason for this masquerade or am I going to have to worm it out of you by cunning?"

Lisa lowered her arm and fingered the brush reflectively. "It was just an impulse." She leveled a thoughtful glance at the other. "Why the sudden interest, Miss Broome?"

"Make it Carla, please," her warm tone made her appeal impossible to resist.

The thought flickered through Lisa's mind that Carla Broome's persuasive powers were disarmingly skillful. She looked over at the lounging figure appraisingly.

"After all, we're going to be shipmates for two weeks," Carla was saying in an amused tone. "You look much more promising than Mrs. Altose or Mr. Rousch. And frankly, so do Dr. Thorson and Mr. McAllister," she concluded with an impish grin that took years off her age. "It's better to get on the right side in the beginning and you obviously have the inside track with them."

"You won't need any help," Lisa told her. "Dr. Thorson is already intrigued and Mr. McAllister . . ."

"What about Mr. McAllister?" Carla asked.

"My recommendation with James McAllister wouldn't get you to first base. Any thoughts you have along that line had better be original."

"My only thoughts regarding the handsome

James would be that he's a good ten years younger than I am, thank you," Carla said pertly. "However, I intend to watch the action with great interest."

"You're wasting your time," Lisa said flatly. "The only action will consist of bored yawns from all concerned."

"If you continue to wear that outfit from the Salvation Army discard barrel, you may be right," Carla told her.

"It is pretty ghastly, isn't it?"

"You've set fashion back forty years on all counts," Carla agreed. "What caused the transformation? Did someone blow the whistle on you?"

"Sandro Ceranini." Lisa started brushing her hair again. "I met him in Los Angeles last year."

"Well, good for Signor Ceranini then," Carla enthused, pushing her short gray hair into the casual style that went so well with her tanned features. "Besides, you couldn't have worn that dress every day."

"I had some other unattractive combinations all planned. The type men like James McAllister expect lady archaeologists to wear."

"Oh ho, so that's it." Carla's laugh bubbled out. "The game is getting more interesting already. Men as big and rugged as Mr. McAllister are entitled to a slight lack of tact. I'll bet he looks terrific in a uniform."

Lisa stiffened. "How did you know he was in the Navy?"

"Somebody must have told me—perhaps it was the purser." Carla seemed unconcerned. "There's the gong for dinner." She pushed over to the end of the bed and stood erect, absently smoothing the skirt of her smart black and white knit. "Why don't you drape a chiffon scarf over your hair and come along?"

Lisa glanced at her reflection with distaste. "No thanks. I'll ask the stewardess to bring me something down here. Now that I've started to get back to normal, I can't wait to shed all this getup."

"All right." Carla smiled at her as she paused by the door. "I'll spread the word upstairs that you haven't jumped overboard or done anything drastic."

The younger woman shrugged. "Whatever you like."

"Cheer up, sweetie, things will look better when you get into some high heels and lipstick. See you later."

"See you," Lisa echoed absently as she watched the door close behind her. Strange that Carla should take such an interest in their doings; perhaps the articles she wrote for her women's magazine were beginning to pall and she hoped for a change of scene.

She wasn't alone in that. After the way her own plan had backfired, any change would be for the better. Of all the ships in the Italian merchant fleet, Sandro would have to be aboard the *Lucarno*. And just when she had James McAllister convinced that his bumptious ideas on intellectual career women were right.

She unearthed a tube of shampoo and started for the bathroom. The best thing to do was to plan a diversionary strategy; remembering the unpleasant look on Jim McAllister's face, it would behoove her to stay out of his way until then.

It was considerably later that evening when Lisa made her way up to the sun deck. Despite the magnificent title, it was actually a small area by the funnel where there was scarcely enough room to parcel out a few wooden deck chairs. At dusk, the deck steward carefully folded them all away, so that nighttime visitors were given a choice of leaning on the rail or perching on a wooden storage locker containing life jackets.

The shaded lightbulbs placed at strategic intervals on the railing were feeble illumination compared to the magnificence of the moon shining down on the calm Mediterranean waters. The land mass that was Italy's east coast had gradually faded into the shadows earlier in the evening, increasing the feeling of isolation aboard ship. There were only the faint navigation lights of a vessel far to port to connect the *Lucarno* with the world of reality. On larger ships, there would have been strains of an or-

chestra playing in the lounge or the footsteps
of passengers strolling the promenade deck to
interrupt the silence. But on the freighter only
the creak of the lines securing the forward deck
cargo could be heard over the regular, if asth-
matic, sound of the engine. The vibration of
the deck beneath her feet indicated that she
must be standing directly over the engine in
question. Lisa grinned suddenly. The *Lucarno*
would have built-in vibrator deck chairs without extra charge, and even a trans-Atlantic
liner couldn't boast that.

She walked across the small sunning space
and put her elbows on the starboard railing,
looking back to admire the reflections on the
water at the stern.

"So this is where you've gotten to."

She froze for a moment and then turned
slowly to face the tall figure at her side. "Did
you come up to gloat, Mr. McAllister, or was
there some insult you forgot to bestow earlier?"

The bright moonlight caught the expression
of unease that passed over his face. "Actually,"
he said, "I came up to apologize."

"Was this all your own idea?" Her tone was
skeptical.

He looked as if he'd been caught still further
off base. "Just partly." A crease of smile appeared. "Adam did some prompting. I probably would have gotten around to it sooner or
later but to be honest, I was still mad as hell at

dinner. And madder still when I found you'd decided to give food a miss. Your absence, together with Adam's lecture on how to behave with a lady, resulted in a massive case of heartburn after the lasagna." His grin became wider. "However, as time went by, both the indigestion and my temper cooled. I hope you had something to eat wherever you were hiding."

"I was not hiding," she retorted as if stung. "I just decided to have dinner in my cabin while my hair was drying."

"Umm." He surveyed her wavy hair, shining like newly minted gold in the moonlight. "I wasn't going to mention it but you're a far cry from that apparition in the lounge this afternoon." He let his glance wander down her smartly fitting white pants suit. "You seem to have shed about twenty years."

"Amazing!" Her tone was still frosty. "You recognized me without a flower in my teeth or . . ."

"Can't we forget that?" he interrupted. "I did apologize."

"So you did. Your interest isn't particularly gratifying, Mr. McAllister. I'm still the same person even though the outer trappings may have varied."

"Come off it, Miss Halliday," he stressed the name mockingly. "I don't know the reason for your disguise, but looking the way you did, Cleopatra couldn't have persuaded Mark Antony to put a foot on her barge. Don't tell me you have some kind of psychiatric hangup about appearing attractive to the opposite sex."

"Of all the conceited apes!" Her anger boiled to the surface. "As if I give a darn what you or any other man thinks about my appearance!"

"Then you are some kind of nut," he drawled. "Even corn flakes sell better if the packaging's attractive."

"And what makes you think I have anything to sell to you?" The voice became dangerously level.

"Oh for lord's sake, stop acting like little Nell caught out in the storm." He stuck a cigarette in the corner of his mouth and used his lighter successfully despite the slight breeze. "You're not selling and I'm certainly not buying, so simmer down." He paused deliberately and then went on. "It's only when people get to know each other very well indeed that they can dispense with the trappings and tinsel. In the meantime, you can give me an inkling of why you were running around looking like Mother Machree."

She looked up at him defiantly. "That's what you expected, wasn't it? All lady archaeologists look as if somebody dug them up by mistake and they should be pushed back down in the hole again."

Her remark hung in the air between them.

He stared at her, momentarily disconcerted, his forehead creased in thought. Then he grinned. "I'll be damned—so you were listening this afternoon. . . . Of course! The lady looking in the glove shop behind us." Broad shoulders shook with silent laughter. "I was admiring you. Now I know why you walked away so fast; it serves you right for eavesdropping."

"I was not eavesdropping," she flashed. "And I hate generalizations like yours."

"I don't see why you should. Obviously you're not the tennis shoe type."

"There you go again." She threw up her hands helplessly. "You haven't the foggiest idea what type I am."

He leaned back with both elbows braced on the rail. "We have two weeks to find out, haven't we?"

She edged a slight distance away from him defensively. "You forget that we have other things to do."

"I'm not forgetting anything. With any luck, Rousch won't sober up for a couple of days so we can relax until Iskanderun."

"What about Brindisi?"

He shook his head. "You're not up on the latest scheduling. The purser told us at dinner that they're skipping Brindisi this voyage. The freight commitments call for them to head straight for Turkey."

"I didn't know they could do that. What if some of the passengers had other plans?"

"Too bad. Actually, no one is being inconvenienced, but if you read the small print on your ticket, you'd find that the captain can make any schedule changes he chooses."

She smiled fleetingly as she gazed toward the water. "Only lawyers read fine print."

"Um. Maybe that's why we're such an unhappy breed. At any rate, the *Lucarno* loses money on every passenger she carries."

"Then why on earth do they bother?"

"For docking privileges. Ships carrying passengers in the Mediterranean are given immediate berths at the various ports of call. Freighters without passengers can be stuck out in the harbors of the busier ports for some time. If you can guarantee time of arrival for freight consignments, the prime rate goes up. So for profits, the shipping company is willing to put up with passengers."

"But the passengers just lost out on Brindisi."

"Maybe they'll sail close enough to shore for you to wave as we go past," he suggested blandly.

She turned to face him. "It's merely that I wanted to see the entrance to the old harbor; I'd read that it was unusual."

"I thought you were just interested in tombs."

Her sigh was resigned. "You certainly have a one-track mind concerning women in my line of work. Would it help any to say that I almost switched to an English major, or would that erect some other horrible image in your mind?"

"Probably. At least, you're not a legal eagle. That would be too much when I'm over here."

"I'm glad I've managed to please you in something; it would have kept me awake nights otherwise." The sarcasm was heavy in her voice and she gave him a brief, scathing look. "You've done your duty now so why don't you leave me alone. I have no feelings of remorse over my brief masquerade and no intention of jumping overboard, so you can depart with a clear conscience."

"Oh, I'll see you back to your stateroom," he said casually, completely disregarding her feelings on the subject. "Your Italian friend was pulled into the game so I'm off the hook for tonight."

"What game and what hook?"

Jim raised his eyebrows. "What grammar!" His cigarette was carefully extinguished in an ash container on the rail before he continued. "The bridge game. It turns out that the *Lucarno*'s captain, or Il Supremo as Adam calls him, is a bridge nut. Adam and I were pressed into a rubber even before the after-dinner coffee was served. The purser lassoed Carla to make a fourth. At least, there's no chatter after the hand is played. Il Supremo knows about fifteen words of English and Carla knows the same in Italian. The bidding's part sign language and the only other communication is a snort of disgust if someone trumps the captain's ace. Your pal Ceranini wandered by a few minutes ago while I was dummy and was poleaxed into taking my place."

"If you did the persuading, poleaxed is probably the right word."

McAllister shook his head sadly. "I can see yours is not a forgiving nature—and I came along to make my apologies so nicely."

"Probably because you were curious to see if there were ankles beneath those lisle stockings."

An indolent look was directed that way. "Probably." He rubbed the back of his neck. "If you must insult me, let's go down a deck. This deck has been vibrating under my feet so long that I feel as if I were getting some sort of a seizure."

She moved her elbow away from his proprietary hand. "All right. I was about to turn in, anyway."

"I didn't say you had to retreat to your cabin." He peered down at his watch. "It's the mere shank of the evening, and early bedtimes went out with your former image. Be careful of those stairs," his grip felt like iron on her wrist, "they're so darned steep you could break your neck on them."

Lisa suffered herself to be led. "I'm being careful." She noted the deserted promenade and boat deck as they came to the bottom of the stair. "It looks as if we're the only ones still up, unless the others are in the lounge."

He shook his head. "I shouldn't think so. We

saw Frau Witten and her son at dinner. They're strictly the 'early to bed' type."

"How can you tell?"

"She's about fifty pounds overweight and hasn't been excited about anything except calories for the last ten years. The son's a chip off the old block who consumed a side order of spaghetti along with his lasagna. The chef's going to lose money this trip." Jim sat on the corner of a storage chest. "I'll bet the Wittens are safely tucked away with dreams of sugar plums on the breakfast menu."

"And the Altoses?"

"They were in the bar for an after dinner drink and then headed below." His sudden grin was triumphant. "Carla confirmed that they're honeymooning, so we're not apt to be overloaded with their company. Although, I don't think love has interfered with his appetite, from the amount of food he stashed away at dinner."

Lisa shivered slightly in the breeze and turned her jacket collar up as she moved to get behind the protection of a piece of deck canvas. "I can see where I'm going to have to be careful what I eat or you'll be psychoanalyzing me."

"No extra charge. Lady archaeologists get a special rate." His gaze became intent. "Did you ever want to work in something a little faster moving than your field?"

"I'm not in the witness chair, Mr. McAllister," she said defensively. "My work has a lot more to do with the awarding of grants and record keeping than actual excavation. That's why this jaunt sounded intriguing. I've wanted to see some of these Mideastern digs ever since I was in college."

He shook his head sadly. "You may be wearing chiffon," he nodded toward the flame-colored scarf protruding from her jacket pocket, "but you've got a mind that's wrapped solidly in gray flannel."

"Then don't waste your time trying to penetrate it." The breeze lifted a lock of her hair and she pushed it back in place. "I'm going to bed. Good night, Mr. McAllister."

His tone was casual. "Good night, Miss Halliday."

Stung by his indifference, she pushed her way past the heavy foyer door before he could move to assist her and hurried past the lounge and card room. The last thing she wanted at that moment was any further masculine conversation. She chewed her lower lip. Of all the bone-headed, obstinate creatures, the one named McAllister took the prize! Between his unfriendly sarcasm and Albert Rousch's drunken state, the trip was taking on the allure of the *Titanic*'s maiden voyage.

She started down the curving central stair toward the stateroom deck only to pull up short when she reached the bottom step. Simultaneously, her eyes began prickling and watering from the sudden haze of blue smoke seeping under the door of a forward stateroom and filling the corridor with the acrid fumes. She started toward the cabin and then hesitated, wondering if she should go for help instead. The decision was abruptly taken from her hands by James's appearance on the stairs behind her. He too paused halfway down and then eliminated the bottom steps in a flying leap as he took in the situation in the corridor.

Stopping only long enough to reach in a storage door with a red light over it and grab a fire extinguisher, he ordered, "Hurry up, Lisa. Find a steward or go up and drag Il Supremo away from his card table. I'll need help." He was rattling the locked door knob of the cabin as he spoke. "Come on, open up in there!"

There was no answer, and McAllister's face became grimmer as the smoke billowed up. He moved back and put up a foot to force the lock.

"Whose stateroom is it?" Lisa's voice sounded thin and frightened.

There was a resounding thud as Jim battered at the door, which vibrated in the jamb but still held firmly. He stepped back in the narrow corridor for another onslaught. "The cabin belongs to our friend Rousch," he snarled. "If you don't go and get some help—he'll be the late Mr. Rousch, and Operation Shadrach will be over before it starts."

Lisa fled up the stairs without waiting to hear any more.

CHAPTER FOUR

"I thought you wouldn't make breakfast to-day," Jim said to Lisa the next morning as he stood to pull out her chair, waving away an attentive waiter in the process.

She paused before she sat down, her eyes wandering around the almost deserted dining salon. "It's so late, I almost didn't chance it. Has Dr. Thorson eaten already?"

"Some time ago. Adam's the original sun lover. He left word that he could be found in a deck chair for the rest of the morning." Jim sat down and reached for the coffee pot. "I can recommend the omelet, but skip the toast unless you like it hard and cold."

She raised an eyebrow at his authoritative tone; evidently the man was even in the habit of making insignificant decisions for his female companions. Best to stop that at the beginning. "I hate eggs for breakfast," she told him casually before turning to the hovering waiter and ordering juice, toast, and coffee.

"Good luck," James said briefly, reaching for a roll and the marmalade jar. "I'm glad to see you didn't suffer any ill effects from last night's excitement."

Since Lisa had spent the better part of a half hour selecting a flattering blue linen dress to wear and making sure her makeup would pass the sternest scrutiny, his tepid compliment was a bitter blow. "Why should I?" she said, keeping her voice casual. "After all, I didn't do anything except find a steward to help you."

He took a sip of coffee. "The smoke was pretty thick by then. I thought it might have bothered you."

She shook her head and watched him spread marmalade on a piece of roll. "It obviously didn't affect you or your appetite."

The barely hidden disdain in her tone stopped his hand halfway to his mouth. He stared at her dispassionately before proceeding. "If the smoke didn't get you, then the lack of sleep did. Or are you always in such a grim mood before breakfast?" He pushed the coffee pot her way. "Here, better have some of this."

She compressed her lips, annoyed at the fugitive gleam of laughter in his eyes. "I am perfectly all right and this conversation is ridiculous. All I really want to know is how Rousch is."

"As of a half hour ago, our friend was sleeping like a baby." The blandness of his voice indicated that he was one male who knew when to pander to the vagaries of an unreasonable female. "Earlier, he borrowed some aspirin from the steward, complained of a monumental hangover, and went back to sleep."

"Did he remember any of the excitement?"

"The steward didn't say. After Rousch was dragged out of the cabin last night, he just opened his eyes long enough to complain about the bright lights and then passed out again. He must have been so sozzled the smoke didn't have a chance."

Lisa finished her juice and surveyed the napkin-covered dish that had just been placed in front of her. Pulling off the wrappings gingerly, she discovered a pile of wedge-shaped pieces of bread that must have been toasted the day before to achieve such a rock-like solidity. Trying to hide her dismay, she attempted to tear off the corner of the top slice and ended up clutching it with a wrestler's grip. Only then, did she glance up to see James's expression.

He met her eyes squarely, completely dead pan. "Would you care for the marmalade?"

Lisa's pride shattered like an icicle falling from a roof. "I'd rather have one of your rolls, if you don't mind."

Silently, he passed her the plate. "Help yourself. The waiter will bring more if we run out. Will it bother you if I smoke?"

She shook her head. "Not a bit. I still can't understand how even a drunk could escape the consequences of smoke inhalation."

"He was lucky enough to fall asleep with the porthole open."

"But they're not supposed to be open—because of the air conditioning. There's a printed warning about it."

"I know that," he spoke kindly but distinctly, as if dealing with a retarded child, "but the fact remains that they can be opened easily. Lots of people prefer the fresh air to air conditioning. Apparently Rousch fits in that category. Until he sobers up, that's all we can surmise."

She reached for the butter. "The way he looked last night, that should be about the time we get to Turkey—if we're lucky. Do they know what caused the fire?"

He nodded. "Probably a cigarette in the overturned waste basket by the door. The hall rug was smoldering when we broke in."

"It's fortunate he wasn't smoking in bed."

"If," he paused suggestively, "Rousch was the one who was smoking."

She frowned and stared across the table. "But the door was locked."

"It can be locked from either side. On the *Lucarno* they make it easy for you." Seeing her puzzled look he continued. "Take a look in the corridor by the steward's cubicle. All the stateroom keys are hung on a board there. We have nothing to prove that Rousch did or did not have a visitor earlier in the evening." He scratched the top of his nose. "If you want to get rid of a body, this is the ship for it. Nobody sees anything from six P.M. on. There's one night steward for the entire ship and he spends most of his time down in the crew's quarters." He shook his head. "I've heard of a casual approach to things, but this is ridiculous. We'll be lucky if we can even find out when Rousch leaves the ship, let alone know what's happening in the meantime."

She made a grimace of sympathy. "I see what you mean. But surely, he hasn't been fool enough to bring the jewelry with him."

"I wouldn't think so. From the way Adam described that golden collar, it wasn't the sort of thing you can carry around in your pants pocket." He looked up to see her staring toward the far side of the room. "Now what?"

She flushed and transferred her gaze hastily back. "Sorry, I got carried away at the amount of food that child is stowing away. He's on his third egg at the moment."

James chuckled but did not turn around. "Sounds like Frau Witten and her son Kurt."

"A woman with a severe Dutch bob ... about forty."

"And a young towhead about five by five." He nodded. "Adam and I nicknamed him B.B. after watching him plough through dinner last night."

"B.B.?"

"Blubber boy. He's going to eat his weight before he leaves the ship. Like the old Aga Khan equaling his in precious stones. The purser will be poised on the rail when he sees the food bill."

Lisa kept tabs on the food disposal under discreetly lowered lids. "At least B.B. comes by it naturally; his mama has the same tendencies."

"Probably eats to cover a broken heart," James assured her. "If I had to pay that young man's grocery bill, I'd be stricken too. Speaking of food," he said as he helped himself to another roll, "I may as well keep you company."

She eyed his lean frame severely. "Keep on that way with the starches and your uniform won't fit when you get back to Naples."

"I'll be taking it off in Florida in another week or so and I can diet all winter." He extinguished his cigarette and pushed the ash tray to one side. "Your chum Mr. Altose isn't any slouch in the food department either."

"He is not my chum."

"No, that's right. Signor Ceranini is the one who comes in that category, isn't he?" James felt his tone take on a cutting edge and deliberately held himself in check. "He feels that finding you aboard was an unexpected bonus. That is, if it *was* unexpected."

The inference made her pause and then resume eating slowly. Only the faint tremor of her hands showed that his shaft had scored. "Quite unexpected, I assure you," she dabbed at her lips with her napkin and pushed her plate back, "but not altogether unpleasant. If you'll excuse me . . ."

"Just a minute." The sudden coolness in his voice matched hers. "You can be helpful today if Rousch emerges from his cocoon."

"In what way?"

"I want a chance to investigate his cabin. If he should get up to the lounge or sun deck, I'd appreciate your help in keeping him there. Adam's promised to keep an eye out for the same thing."

She pushed back her chair and stood up. "Very well. Consider it done, Lieutenant McAllister."

He watched her trim figure disappear through the archway. "Damn," he said softly, and threw his napkin on the table. For a man who prided himself on being logical, it struck him that his sudden outburst of temper had been highly illogical, to say the least—almost on a par with his anger of the night before. The thought of another apology being due was as bitter as his final swallow of coffee.

From their table, Frau Witten and B.B. watched him stride out of the room and then turned back to their plates without missing a bite.

Jim thrust his hands in the pockets of his slacks and shouldered aside the glass doors into the lounge. The trouble with a ship, he decided, was that there wasn't any place to get away from things. Anybody wanting to walk off a bad temper would end up getting dizzy from taking too many turns around the short deck. And as far as escaping into real isolation, the closest land was about six hundred feet straight down, according to the chart on the wall. That left three choices: to hole up in his cabin, join the sun worshippers of the deck chair brigade, or sit in sulky grandeur in the lounge. He chose the latter and strolled over to the bar where a crewman was arranging bottles.

"Something for the signore?"

"*Espresso, per favore.*"

"*Si.*" The man turned to the gleaming coffee machine and started turning knobs.

"My lord, imagine finding you hunched over the bar at breakfast time. I didn't think you'd become such a dissolute character as that." Adam, clad in a noisy sports shirt and a pair of disreputable khaki shorts, slid onto a bar stool next to him. "Is this a rehearsal to get you in the mood for associating with our overweight friend?"

"If you want a cup of espresso say so," Jim growled. "Otherwise, spare me the humor."

"I'd swear you hadn't had breakfast yet if I didn't know better. Getting crochety in your old age?"

The other accepted a steaming cup of coffee before answering. "Come on, let's go over to a chair and sit in comfort. My old age, as you call it, has convinced me that I'm past the period of sitting on bar stools."

They made their way to a table by the long windows overlooking the bow and sank into upholstered chairs.

"This is more like it," Adam said gratefully. "The pads on the deck chairs leave a lot to be desired." He stretched out in comfort. "About three inches more of foam rubber, to be exact."

"So that's what brought you down from the bikini bailiwick."

Thorson shook his head. "I will never convince you that there's more to sun bathing than that."

McAllister allowed himself a brief grin. "Speak for yourself. What else is going on topside?"

"Very little. The Altoses went up with all their impedimenta."

"Impedimenta?"

"Suntan oil, nose guards—the works." Adam looked disgusted. "From the amount of stuff they cart around, you'd think they were going on safari."

"Just because you've got walrus hide doesn't mean—"

"I know, but people like that make a production out of putting on their sunglasses. Anyhow, they're in one corner. Miss Broome is stretched out on a locker."

"In a well-fitting swim suit?"

Adam nodded. "In a well-fitting swim suit, but also tending strictly to her own business.

Our conversation consisted of 'Good morning' and 'Nice day.' "

Jim found himself wishing that he could report the same success at the breakfast table. He took a cautious sip of coffee. "Don't worry, things should improve before lunch."

Adam gave him a whimsical glance. "Possibly you're right, but not with me. Signor Ceranini was arriving to try his luck. I took one look at his muscles and decided I'd better leave. The contrast was terrible."

"There's only one muscle that guy's developed—the thick one in his head."

"You're prejudiced. I take it you've seen Lisa this morning."

"As a matter of fact, I have. We shared a breakfast table."

Thorson raised his eyebrows and leaned back in his chair. "Anything new?"

"We disagreed again, but you could hardly call that new." Jim drained his coffee cup and put it back in the saucer. "She's promised to hang onto Rousch if I ever get a chance to go over his cabin." He pulled an ashtray toward himself. "I'll bet next month's salary that any search will be strictly for exercise. He's too smart to keep anything incriminating around."

"He could have hidden the things somewhere else on the ship."

"Possible," Jim reached for a cigarette and lit it, "but not probable. Not after all these months. At any rate, I should have a chance to check his cabin before we get to Turkey. We dock at Iskanderun early tomorrow morning, don't we?"

Adam nodded. "About six. It's a very interesting place, even these days."

Jim looked across at him. "That's right, you were over here a few years ago, weren't you?"

"During the summer holidays." Adam smiled reminiscently. "Marvelous trip. I was retracing the *Via Dei* of the First Crusade."

"The Way of God." Jim drew deeply on his cigarette and frowned in concentration. "My homework's coming back. Iskanderun was on the main route for the crusaders about nine hundred years ago, wasn't it?"

Thorson nodded. "Although you'd never know it these days. It's just a sleepy little port —quite different from the days when it was named after Alexander the Great. That's what Iskanderun roughly translates into. Alexander's town. Now the natives live on the proceeds from a Mideast pipeline and the commerce from an American air force base about fifty miles away. From a classical point of view, it's a pity."

McAllister grinned. "But scarcely new. They sell snacks in the Parthenon and soft drinks in the Vatican, too."

The professor nodded again. "A sign of the times, I suppose. At any rate, you won't have to dodge through hordes of tourists. The captain was telling me last night that this is one of the few ships to call in."

"That should help keep prices down if the ladies want to go shopping."

Adam flushed slightly. "Miss Broome has already mentioned that. She wondered if I'd take her into the souks, since I'd been here before."

"On the hook, eh? I'm going to enjoy watching you wriggle. It's amazing what can be accomplished between 'good morning' and 'nice day.' "

"The discussion took place last night at the bridge table after you'd made yourself scarce," Adam said with a stab at dignity. He shot a thoughtful look at the younger man. "I can't say this trip has done anything to improve your disposition. Anybody would think you had been auditioning for Scrooge ever since we boarded the ship. You're either sickening for something or someone or . . ."

"Oh, drop it!" Jim's irritated exclamation was cut short as he saw a couple, deep in conversation, at the entrance to the lounge.

Lisa had changed into a sunning costume guaranteed to raise the blood pressure of an octogenarian. For modesty's sake, her brief halter and trim shorts were covered by a fingertip-length jacket. Since the jacket itself was of sheer cotton, however, the overall effect was more tantalizing than concealing. At least, Albert Rousch, who was hovering beside her, seemed to think so.

Jim was across the lounge and into the foyer before Adam could do more than get to his feet.

"Good morning again, Mr. McAllister." Only someone who was listening as intently as Jim could have determined the nervousness underlying Lisa's gay greeting. "Mr. Rousch and I have decided to go up and get some sun." She bestowed a dazzling smile on the pudgy man beside her.

Rousch deigned to acknowledge McAllister's presence. "I met you yesterday, didn't I?" he asked. "The steward says you helped save my life last night. You must accept my thanks."

"It was hardly that," James demurred.

Amazing how much dignity Rousch could attain, standing there in his wrinkled jeans and T-shirt. From the way he was holding his head, the man must have the colossus of all hangovers, as well. This was confirmed by his next utterance.

"I think, Miss Halliday, that a little coffee would be . . ."

"Make it Lisa, please," she interrupted. "We can get coffee up on the sun deck, the steward told me." She took his elbow persuasively. "But we'd better hurry or we'll be too late. Besides," she shivered exaggeratedly, "I'm about to freeze in this air conditioning."

Jim's eyes swept her figure scathingly. "I'm not surprised."

"Nor I." Rousch's beam illuminated his

mottled face. "I meant to tell you how lovely you look, my dear." His hand closed possessively around the fine bones of her wrist. "Let us continue the discussion over our coffee. Excuse us, Mr. McAllister." His bow would have been laughable if it hadn't been done so naturally.

"Yes, excuse us, Mr. McAllister," Lisa mocked before she was ushered out on the deck.

For the moment, James merely stood looking after them.

"You'd better hop down to his cabin," Adam's tone was casual as he came over beside him. "Lisa's doing her part very well but there's no point in making her prolong the dialogue."

"She takes to it naturally, doesn't she?" Jim's words were hardly discernible through his clenched jaws.

"Can't really say." Adam tucked in his shirttail. "I'll go back up to my deck chair and provide her with some reserve strength. Don't be too long, Jim. Rousch looks like the kind who could be skittish, despite Lisa's dressing for the part." He glanced over his shoulder toward the door. "Pretty effective costuming, wasn't it?"

"If you like that sort of thing. The next step on the ladder would be a go-go dancer."

Thorson's glance was bland. "Mata Hari was misunderstood, too."

Jim snorted and turned to the stair.

On the lower deck, he slowed his pace and

made sure the corridor was deserted before he removed Rousch's stateroom key from the board by the steward's quarters. He looked over his shoulder once again in front of Rousch's door and then put his ear to the panel. The only sound seemed to be the reverberation of the *Lucarno*'s engines. Swiftly he inserted the key, turned it, and stepped inside the room. He locked the door behind him, taking care to remove the key and put it in his pocket.

The single stateroom had undergone a thorough housecleaning since the last time he'd been in it. All evidences of the fire were removed, but the faint smell of smoke still hung in the air.

He moved quickly to the closet and pulled out a bulging suitcase, noting that a dark suit was hanging in solitary splendor above it. Since Rousch's wardrobe seemed limited to the suit for formal occasions and his blue jeans for all other events, it was obvious the man didn't spend his money on clothes.

Jim bent over the bag and pushed the catch hopefully. It snapped open to reveal miscellaneous toilet articles and a wrinkled white shirt being used for padding between a bottle of vodka and a bottle of gin. He examined the lining of the suitcase before pushing its contents back in place.

He replaced the bag in the closet and straightened to look around the small room.

Before searching further, he moved quietly to the door; still no sound from the corridor outside. Only then did he move to the metal bureau beside the bed and start checking the drawer contents. Afterwards, the spring and mattress were subjected to the same swift but efficient scrutiny. When it was over, he pulled the spread back to an accurate imitation of its former appearance. He frowned as he went over to check the portholes behind their curtains and then moved into the bathroom. A few moments there sufficed to prove that Rousch hadn't stuffed any priceless antiquities in the holder with the toilet brush or down the bathtub drain.

Jim stiffened as he heard the murmur of voices and steps in the corridor. He remained immobile until the disturbance dwindled and disappeared completely after a nearby door slammed. Then he glanced at his watch; time to get off the premises unless he wanted to push his luck. Trying to explain his presence behind a locked door in the wrong cabin would strain the credulity of even the most informal Italian steward.

He put the key back in the lock, turned it and opened the door cautiously. He took another swift look up and down the corridor before he stepped out and locked the door behind him in a decisive movement. The key was replaced on the community board almost as quickly.

Only then did he breathe a sigh of relief and give thanks to the shipping company for making stateroom keys so available.

Jim stopped off in his cabin long enough to change into a sports shirt and a pair of shorts for the sun deck. As he was transferring his belongings, he grimaced in disgust. Sitting in the sun when there wasn't a swimmng pool aboard was certainly a waste of time, but his appearance would let Adam and Lisa know the search was over.

He closed the door behind him, considered locking it and then grinned briefly. It was hardly worth the trouble, as he could testify from firsthand knowledge. Still grinning, he made his way up to the promenade deck and then up the steep stairs past the bridge to the top deck.

Most of the *Lucarno*'s passenger list was clustered in the deck space allotted to sun bathing. Lisa's deck chair was sandwiched between those of Sandro Ceranini and Albert Rousch. Jim's eyebrows climbed. Talk about a rose between two thorns! In swim trunks, Rousch looked like a sausage with a string around the middle. Ceranini, on the other hand, must have been the star graduate of a muscle-building school. His biceps flexed impressively as he leaned over to put a possessive hand on Lisa's arm. Jim turned his head abruptly in the other direction. From a horizontal perch atop a storage locker, Carla was watching the scene under half-closed lids. The Altoses were stretched on their chairs further amidships, bounded by a circle of lotion bottles and tubes. Near them, Adam lounged by the rail.

He raised a hand in greeting as Jim strolled over to his side. "Pull up a chair."

"Thanks." McAllister glanced at the other's battered straw hat pulled low on his forehead. "Why the head gear?"

"Because my hair isn't as thick as it used to be and I don't like frying my brains just for appearances. Any other questions?"

McAllister, who had expected an answer of this type, merely grinned.

Adam lowered his voice. "I take it that the search party is completed."

"All finished and nary a thing to show for it. Not that we expected there would be." Jim turned his body fractionally to stare over his shoulder. "I see that Lisa is still doing her job."

Thorson looked down at his feet and kept his voice low. "Very effectively. Ceranini joined her party so I didn't volunteer my services. I think Rousch has been trying to get Lisa to himself, but she's not having any."

Jim settled his gaze on the horizon. "The silly woman's going to be parboiled if she doesn't get out of this sun. That thin cotton thing she's got over her shoulders doesn't afford any protection and she's close enough to a red-head to be vulnerable. Always supposing the color of her hair is natural," he added sardonically.

"Well, if it isn't it's a damned good job," Adam said. "Lisa's not going to be the only one suffering," he added, feeling his thigh gingerly. "I'm going down and get some clothes on before lunch. Shall I meet you in the lounge?"

"Umm. Shortly. Now that I've made an appearance up here, I'd better stay long enough to make it seem logical."

Thorson nodded and hoisted his lean frame. "Good idea. Besides, you can serve as an unofficial chaperon along with Carla. That woman hasn't missed the flick of an eyebrow since I've been up here."

"I wonder what her interest is? She could be gathering copy for an article."

Adam scratched his head, unconsciously moving his hat to a jaunty side angle in the process. "She's gathering something. Otherwise she would have been more relaxed about the whole business, like the Altoses." He gave them a whimsical glance. "There must be something in this honeymoon business, they wouldn't have noticed if we'd hit an iceberg."

"You'll have to try it sometime, Professor."

"The honeymoon or hitting an iceberg?" Thorson realized the way his thoughts were leading and caught himself up. "One's about as likely as the other. I'd better get changed. See you at lunch if not before," he said quickly and went below.

Shortly after Adam left, Carla sat up, pulled the straps of her black swimsuit into place and came over, dragging her chair pad behind her. "Could you stand some company?" she asked in a deliberately plaintive tone.

"Sure, any time." Jim swung his feet down and reached over to put her pad atop Adam's chair. "A little more cushioning helps. It's a pity the shipping company doesn't approve of foam rubber; my bones are grinding on these wooden chair frames."

"That's because you haven't any natural padding. Be thankful." Carla settled herself beside him and pulled a pair of sun glasses from her tote bag. Adjusting them carefully on her nose, she leaned back to let the sun shine directly on her face. "About five minutes more before I'll have to give up like Professor Thorson," she said. "He has everything timed down to a gnat's eyebrow, including the minutes he doesn't spend chatting with females lurking to waylay him."

"Were you waylaying?"

"I was trying to and not getting anywhere. For all the attention I rated, I might as well have been one of the lifeboats."

Jim forebore mentioning that Adam had other things on his mind. "The prof's not much of a one for taking the initiative," he said easily.

"Unlike a younger friend of his," she said just as easily.

"Unlike a younger friend of his," he concurred. "That doesn't mean he isn't interested, just that the approach has to be subtle."

"Ouch!" Carla pushed her glasses further up on the bridge of her nose and gave him a wry look. "That's the trouble with the educational types; a woman has to use her head along with the more obvious things." She let her glance rest on the trio by the rail. "Perhaps I could take lessons from Lisa."

Jim's expression froze. "Adam is a different type from those two lugs."

"Help—I'm getting in deeper." Her tanned hand patted his arm reassuringly. "I didn't mean that the way it sounded. Without even trying, Lisa has her friend Sandro and Mr. Rousch practically snapping at each other. It will be interesting to see which one gets her company for lunch."

"Speaking of food," Jim glanced at his watch, "if we're going to get changed and have time for me to buy you a drink before the gong, we'd better get moving. I promise to give you all the scoop on how to fascinate the professor over something tall and cold."

Carla didn't resist, although her gaze fixed on him speculatively as she stood up beside him. "I suppose there's some method in your madness but it's definitely the best offer I've had all morning, so I'm going to snap you up on it."

Jim made a point of ignoring the cozy threesome in the corner as he followed Carla down the steps. After all, if Miss Halliday had wanted to be rescued, she could have made an excuse to join Adam long before. It battered on the fringe of his consciousness that she could have come over to join him, as well. Perhaps the greatest irritation was the niggling thought that Lisa had no desire to be rescued, that she had happily gone out beyond her depth with Sandro Ceranini and liked it that way.

CHAPTER FIVE

Jim had always read that the greatest disadvantage of traveling on freighters was that the few passengers were constantly thrown into each other's company. It took him the rest of the afternoon, the cocktail hour, and finally dinner to decide that Lisa must have read the same book and was deliberately setting out to prove the fallacy of its contents.

During lunch, she had forsaken the dining room for a deck snack next to the shuffleboard court. For one who was supposed to be grinding her teeth at her choice of companions, she was perversely in the best of spirits as she drank beer with Rousch and hovered over a plate of antipasto with Ceranini. In the dining room, Jim ate undercooked spaghetti with clam sauce and bored Adam with a discourse on why women should not compete in the business world.

Afternoon found Lisa in slacks at the ping pong table on the afterdeck with Ceranini, who was obviously a past master at that game as well. James observed the other man's serve as he strolled by and declined frigidly when pressed to join the game. "Thanks no," he said tersely, "I haven't played since college." He neglected to say that he had shown very little talent for the game even then.

"Sandro tells me he won the championship at his club in Beirut last year," Lisa said, still breathing heavily from a fast rally.

"I'm sure of that," James said, preparatory to strolling on. "You'd better put on a hat, your nose is getting red."

Unfortunately, Sandro's gallant answer penetrated as he walked away. "Ignore him, *cara mia*. With a pink nose, you look like a particularly enticing bunny."

That remark was enough to send James to his cabin with a thick book for the rest of the afternoon. He was pleased to note that the heroine died a tragic death in the fifth chapter.

The fact that Lisa was missing at cocktails was again irritating but hardly alarming. Her absence at dinner, however, started nudging his hard-boiled conscience.

"Where in the hell do you suppose she is now?" he finally asked Adam after fidgeting through the first two courses.

"Who knows?" Adam peered over the top of his glasses. "She is on the legal side of twenty-one and she is entitled to a modicum of privacy. Rousch is at his table inhaling noodles so we can't suspect him. Apparently his day in the fresh air made him decide to consume something solid. Maybe the man's reforming."

"I'll believe that when he starts wearing socks to dinner," Jim said, looking over at Rousch. "He must be having a contest with Altose to see who can take bigger bites of pasta. Even Mrs. A. looks slightly disillusioned."

Adam took a casual look over his shoulder. "If they're having a contest, they should let Frau Witten's son in on it. He's got a platterful that the chef must have been saving for tomorrow's lunch."

"She should be having something to eat."

"Who . . . Frau Witten? She's not suffering."

"I meant Lisa," Jim snapped. "One of us should find out what's wrong."

Adam shook his head. "No thanks. Not until you can convince me that something is wrong. Maybe you haven't noticed that Ceranini's among the missing, too."

"What kind of an insinuation is that? You don't think she's making that creep's company a substitute for dinner!"

"Since you're in such a miserable mood, the same thought has obviously occurred to you. Why don't you ask Carla? She's eating over at the purser's table."

James shook his head slowly to reject the idea. "I'd feel an almighty fool." He plunged his spoon into some spumoni and then pushed it away. "You're probably right. Lisa'll turn up, dragging her Italo-Lebanese sheep behind her."

Adam took a swallow of wine. "Are you playing bridge tonight?"

"No thanks. Tell Leon to round up another volunteer. Carla said she'd play if you needed her."

"Did she?" A look of mild interest went over Adam's thin face. "So much bridge seems a little tame for anyone like her."

"Maybe you've been misled," Jim reproved. "The label is not always the proper advertisement for the contents—rule number one in the bachelor's handbook. If Il Supremo screams for a fourth, the purser can oblige."

"Where are you off to?"

The other grinned slightly. "Well, you can be sure of one thing, it won't be far away."

Jim managed to spend the next three hours strolling about without raising too many curious glances. The bridge game was the top social event of the evening, with Il Supremo grumbling because Leon had been pressed into service. Frau Witten and B.B. disappeared down to their cabin, presumably for bedtime snacks and to dream of more treats for breakfast. The Altoses occupied two chairs close together on the sun deck and obviously considered their position out of bounds for anyone else. After one stroll by, Jim decided to leave them in solitude, confining his meanderings to the lower decks. Rousch was consuming vodka in the bar with the stewards making bets about how long it would be before he passed out.

Only Sandro Ceranini and Lisa remained among the missing. Jim stayed aloof until ten-thirty, when his last resolutions vanished. At that time, he found himself in front of Lisa's cabin door deliberately putting his ear against the metal, cursing himself for all kinds of a fool as he did it.

Silence reigned and he was about to take his head away when he heard a whimper and then broken sobbing. He straightened with a grim look on his face and then bent to listen again. Finally, a frown creasing his forehead, he strode back down the deserted corridor and through the serviceway to the other side of the ship.

He was back at her door within three minutes. This time he knocked.

There was a faint rustle inside and finally Lisa's voice sounding plaintive. "Go away— I don't know how to say it in Italian."

Jim's jaws tightened but he merely reached down, opened the door and stepped into the hallway. The dim illumination from a light on the dressing table revealed her huddled form on the bed.

"Good evening," he said in an expressionless voice. "I thought I'd better find out what had become of you."

"Oh!" Lisa started to jump up, but she winced and drew in a sharp breath of pain.

Ignoring her mutinous face, he strode forward and put the burden he had been carrying

94

on top of the dressing table. "Before you start screaming, I've brought a chaperon."

Her flushed face crumpled into an unwilling smile. "Shadrach, my favorite beast. I feel honored to get a glimpse of him."

"Damned right. It isn't everyday a camel comes calling."

"Should I ask how Meshach and Abednego are?"

"I'm asking the questions, my girl." He sat down on the edge of her bed. "You really caught the sun on your shoulders, didn't you?"

She nodded. "That's why I'm still wearing this halter. When I try to put on any other clothes, it hurts like the dickens. It's a good thing I changed into slacks after lunch or I'd be a solid mass of misery."

"So you stayed huddled in here crying about it. Of all the idiots on this ship, you take the cake!" He reached in his pocket and pulled out a tube of ointment. "This stuff should help. The U.S. Navy may have strange ideas of what to serve for breakfast, but they're pretty sharp in the medical department." Unscrewing the cap, he went on, "Put your feet down straight and lie on your side with your back to me."

"I can manage."

"I said turn over and I meant it. If you don't cooperate, I'll find a part of your anatomy that isn't sunburned and be more forceful."

"All right. You needn't get so cross."

"The fact that you're a partial invalid is the

only thing that keeps you from a darned good beating, lady. It wasn't necessary to dress like a houri to keep Rousch in attendance."

"I didn't know how much ammunition I needed to do the job."

"My God, with that outfit, you could have kept the entire French foreign legion at bay for the weekend." He put the cap on the dressing table. "I suppose by rights your friend Sandro should be doing the honors."

"What do you mean, by rights?"

"I'd have been to the rescue a lot sooner if I hadn't thought the two of you were . . ."

"Were what?" She had pulled completely away from him and her words came out like slivers of ice. "Or don't you want to finish the sentence? I certainly run the gamut of reputations with you; one day I'm an old crone because of my job and the next I'm practically a scarlet woman because I play ping-pong with a man." Her eyes narrowed. "Why don't you go away and leave me in peace. I liked it better when I just had the sunburn, at least I could try to ignore it."

For a moment it looked as if he would take her at her word. His lips tightened and he half rose from the edge of the bed. Then he sank back down again and shook his head. "Don't tell me I'm going to have to apologize again."

Lisa swallowed the sob that rose in her throat. "What's the matter," she managed tremulously, "afraid of setting a precedent?"

"Maybe," his look was intent. "And of losing future decisions." He took her elbows gently but firmly and turned her back to him once again. "Now lie still and let me get some of this stuff on. It's supposed to stop blistering and peeling."

His hands were gentle as they smoothed the cream over angry red skin, and other than an involuntary gasp when he started, she remained quiet under his touch.

"That's got most of your back," he told her finally. "Now move around and lie flat on your stomach."

Lisa gave him a startled glance, but decided not to argue and followed his orders. She settled her head on the pillow and immediately felt his fingers unfastening her halter at the neckline.

"What are you doing?" she squeaked, struggling up on her elbows and then hastily dropping back down again.

"Simmer down," he said with amusement, "I can't work around straps and harnesses. As long as you stay flat, all conventions are satisfied— Shadrach will see to that."

"I'm quite sure this isn't in the chapter on chaperones," she said, hoping that he couldn't feel the trip-hammer beat of her heart, which seemed to be functioning in double time. Despite her nervousness, his gentle, soothing strokes felt marvelously cool on her smarting flesh and she gradually relaxed under the pressure of his hands.

"That's wonderful," she said drowsily, "you ought to hang out a shingle."

"Umm." The motion stopped abruptly. "That should do it," he said roughly. "Put yourself back together while I wash this salve off my hands. I want to talk to you."

She felt the mattress spring back from his weight as he stood up and went into the bathroom, closing the door firmly behind him. Lisa fastened her halter and then stood to run a comb through her tousled hair. Her reflection showed a pale face still bearing evidences of tear stains. Hastily she rubbed her cheeks to try and dispel the telltale signs. Then, hearing the bathroom door open, she sank onto the edge of the bed.

Jim walked over and sat down in the metal chair by the footboard. Silently he offered her a cigarette and, as she shook her head, put his lighter flame to the end of his.

"Feeling better?" he asked tersely.

"Yes thanks, much." She balled the pillow behind her and sat scrunched up by the headboard. "You can't be very comfortable on that chair."

He didn't bother to deny her statement. "It's safer here. I didn't think about occupational hazards when I came on my errand of mercy."

"Hazards?" Her eyes widened.

"Weren't you aware of them? Strange—I

could have sworn you were." He watched her cheeks flush before he deliberately changed the subject. "What did you find out from Rousch today?"

She took a deep breath and let it out slowly. "Not too much," she said evenly. "The man has incredible conceit."

"In what way?"

"He's convinced he's God's gift to women. Evidently he spent enough time in Damascus to embrace Moslem ideas toward the female sex."

"Such as . . ."

"Well, he's for quality as well as quantity, but if he has to give up one . . ."

"He'll take quantity."

"How did you know?"

"My lord, girl, you don't have to live in Damascus to figure out somebody like Rousch."

She started to shrug her shoulders and stopped midway with a pained grimace. "All right, so you're better at character analysis than I am." The pillow was pushed into a more comfortable position and she leaned back gingerly. "I found out something else—Herr Rousch doesn't smoke."

"No fooling." James whistled silently. "So the fire last night wasn't of his doing."

Lisa shook her head. "I don't think so, at least, not from a cigarette. He didn't want to talk about it. I couldn't tell whether he was embarrassed by all the fuss or something else."

"Stop being devious and come to the point."

"All right," she said defensively. "If you want an opinion that is strictly feminine intuition, I'd say he was frightened."

McAllister's eyebrows went up. "I hadn't thought of that angle. If you're right, then he must have recognized somebody on board who knows about his role in all this."

"Um hum." She wrapped her arms around her drawn-up knees. "Does it occur to you that we're doing a lot of supposing in all this?"

"Constantly." He let his eyes dwell on her. Where Lisa had noted only a pale complexion and tear stains, James saw delicate, high cheekbones and candid eyes framed by thick lashes. The mouth that had once seemed too firm was quirked in a shy smile that would make a robot look twice. He felt his breathing quicken, forcibly aware that his "strictly business" resolve was in danger of crumbling. Deliberately he stood up and said, "I'd better get out of here and let you get some rest. Think you'll be able to sleep now?"

Lisa could recognize the "off" signal as well as any woman. "Of course," she said brightly, thinking that she wouldn't ask for further help from him if she were writhing on the floor. "Don't let me keep you."

Her urging made James more uncomfortable in his resolve than ever, also more perverse. "I wouldn't," he advised stiffly, "plan to do any more entertaining tonight if I were you."

If he'd waved a red flag in a bull ring, he wouldn't have gotten a better response.

"I don't believe I sent out invitations for your visit," she began.

"Oh lord," he groaned, "here comes the lecture. I've done it again."

"You certainly have. With your diplomatic finesse, I'm surprised that the U.S. Navy hasn't declared war on Italy since you've been stationed there."

His eyes glinted with amusement. "The admiral keeps a pretty short leash on me."

"I can see why." She was having trouble hanging onto her anger. "Just keep on the way you're going, Lieutenant McAllister, and you'll have Shadrach draped in pieces over your ears next time. You've forgotten him, by the way."

"No, I haven't. He's on lend-lease for the moment. I'll reclaim him later." He paused by the door. "We're supposed to dock at Iskanderun fairly early. Since it's a minor Turkish seaport without an air teminal, I doubt if Rousch will try anything there."

Lisa decided to go along with his change of mood. "He didn't look the least interested when Sandro mentioned the town. Apparently there isn't much to see."

"It all depends on what you're looking for. If you haven't made other plans, do you want to go ashore with me?"

"I'd love to." Her quick response was startling even to her ears, and her eyes dropped in confusion before the sudden triumph in his. "What about Dr. Thorson?" she asked hurriedly.

"Let him find his own date. Besides, he's been here before so he's planning to go into town and see what the bazaars offer." He didn't miss her sudden flicker of interest. "You'll have plenty of time to spend money later on in Syria and Lebanon. Tomorrow, you can look at a crusader's castle with me."

She managed a mock salute. "Aye aye, sir. One crusader's castle coming up." Simultaneously, she noted James's intent gaze and became aware of his rugged masculinity in the confines of the tiny hallway. Propinquity was a force to be reckoned with. She took an involuntary step backward, which brought her up against the closet door. Her heartbeat quickened and her eyes clung to his. The spider and the fly, or was it a shark and a minnow? Later, she was unable to remember whether he had taken a step toward her when suddenly there was knocking on the door.

"Lisa, b'yootiful Lisa—I mus' talk to you, cariss'ma," Sandro's heavily accented voice came from the outer corridor.

"Oh lord, he'll wake the ship," Lisa whispered, horrified.

James gave her a resigned glance. "He certainly will. Were you expecting him?"

"I was not. Not now or any time." Her eyes glinted. "What does it take to convince you?"

"You must admit the evidence stacks up."

"Purely circumstantial, believe it or not."
Her expression was as steely as his.

"Lisa, lemme in," Ceranini yodeled.

"If I don't, the entire passenger list will be
down here," she whispered urgently.

"And if you do, you'll have a hell of a lot
more than you can handle," James warned her.
"He sounds completely stoned."

The fist knocked on the door again, louder
this time. "Come on, Lisa mia ... wake up,
wake up and lemme in. We're invited to a
party."

James opened the bathroom door and
stepped inside. He flicked out the hall light so
that the only illumination in the cabin filtered
out from the bedroom beyond. "Go on," he
urged softly, "let him in."

"But what are you going to do?" The knocking had become a thunderous pounding as Lisa
moved forward to unlock the door.

Sandro lurched in when the door opened.
"Lisa, b'yootiful Lisa." He stood swaying
slightly in front of her. "How could you desert
me tonight when I needed you? The crew's
havin' a party—it's still goin' on." His eyes
finally focused on her to take in her abbrevi-
ated costume. "C'mere baby, closer to me." He
lunged forward a step and caught hold of her
sunburned shoulder.

"Ooooh!" She let out a muffled moan as she
tried to get out of his way, and then Sandro was

103

swung around and there was the dull sound of flesh hitting flesh as Jim's fist connected with the other's jaw and Sandro sagged unconscious onto the floor at their feet.

"How could you!" she squeaked.

"I just tapped him," Jim muttered. "He was so loaded that a pygmy could have done the same thing. Now I have to get him out of here." He stepped over the inert form and poked his head out into the hallway. "Good! There's nobody around."

"Are you sure he's breathing?"

"If you have any doubts, I'll leave him here until he comes around and you can explain it all to him."

"Don't be such a beast," she flared.

"Then you'd better get it across to this bag of muscles that you're not in the mood for his parlor tricks." He pushed her aside and reached down to grasp the unconscious man under the arms to pull him out into the hall.

"What are you going to do with him?"

"Prop him up against his stateroom door. When he wakes up, he can go on from there."

"You're sure he's all right?" She caught his disgusted look. "I just don't want you to get into any trouble," she said defensively.

"Let me worry about that. Look, I've got to get him out of here. Lock your door and don't open it again for anybody. Call my stateroom if you need anything . . . anything," he reiterated. "Understand?"

"I understand," she said faintly.

"Now go to bed," he whispered from the hallway as he got a firmer grasp on Ceranini and started to pull him away. "I'll see you in the morning."

"All right." She resisted the urge to peep out to follow his progress down the hall. Only when she had the key turned firmly in the lock did she lean her forehead against the cool metal as her thoughts ran amok. Finally, just before she climbed onto her bed, she reached over to pat the glass camel peering so intently at her from the dressing table.

"Good night, Shadrach," her fingers lingered affectionately on the disdainfully curved nose. "You might note that I'm following orders and give a favorable report." She was still smiling gently as she turned out the light.

Soft early sunlight pouring through Lisa's curtains the next morning provided her with an excuse to move cautiously from her bed and stand erect, wincing as she moved her shoulder muscles under the still-tender skin.

She went over to peer through the porthole and noted the green hills of the Turkish mainland looming large on the horizon. Cotton-batting clouds nestled carelessly in the magnificent blue sky, a gentian blue once found, according to the poets, only over fabled Greek isles. Green foothills in the distance appeared artificial, needing the brown dirt and gray rock outcroppings on their sides to provide a semblance of authenticity. Far overhead, the silver body of a jet reflected brilliantly in the sunshine for a moment and then disappeared to leave only the feathery wisp of a vapor trail.

Lisa smiled, wondering what the leaders of Turkish camel caravans thought these days when their historical heritage plodded behind them and the harbingers of the future winged overhead.

Glancing at the clock on the dressing table, she noted that it was later than she thought; if she was to have an adequate bath before the breakfast gong, she'd better get moving.

Once the taps were turned on and the tub was filling, she gazed in the mirror at the still-reddened skin on her shoulders. The forest fire look was gone, she decided, but a hands-off policy was definitely the order of the day. Fortunately, she had brought a strapless bra; thus she could avoid constricting and painful shoulder straps. Her wrap-around linen skirt with a matching blouse should satisfy Mideast etiquette and pamper her sunburn as well.

She stepped into tepid, perfumed water and was glad that someone had seen fit to provide her with a tub rather than a shower. Needle-like jets of water from a shower head onto her tender shoulders would have had her wailing like a banshee. On the other hand, bubble bath frothing about those same shoulders was luxury indeed. It took a strong will and an eventually guilty conscience to force her to abandon her lazing and rise from the depths. You're a Sybarite, my girl, she told herself as she wielded a fluffy towel carefully.

Whatever medication James had slathered on had certainly helped; the pain of the burn had subsided drastically overnight. It was maddening to have to add first aid prowess to the man's other attributes.

Administering a final pat with the towel, Lisa put it back on the brass wall hook and turned to her clothing, which was piled neatly on the three-legged bath stool. She eased into her bra and then pulled on briefs and a half-slip with more assurance. The ivory-colored blouse and skirt were as flattering as any shade could be with her heightened skin tones, and she confined color accents to a pair of aqua walking pumps and matching bag. Fortunately, her bare legs were tanned already and had not suffered in yesterday's carelessness. She pulled her hair back in a loose chignon low on her neck. The severity of the style threw her cheekbones into prominence and added a new fragility to her expression. She thought about changing to another hairdo, decided against it, and then relaxed, outlining her lips in pale lipstick and using a dab of solid cologne on the inside of her wrists. Finally, checking to see that she had her sunglasses and a soft-brimmed hat along, she made her way up to the dining salon.

Jim, Adam, and Carla were having a final cup of coffee at a table for four in the corner.

"That's what I call a remarkable recovery," Adam told her heartily as both men got to their feet at Lisa's approach.

She made a wry face as she sat down. "You make me sound like something that came back from the dead."

Carla smiled across at her. "If I ever come back from the dead, I hope I can look just like you."

"Nicely put, Carla," Jim said laconically, settling back in his chair. "Better than my heavy-handed friend here."

"My dear fellow," Adam protested, "you insisted that Lisa was suffering from a very bad case of sunburn—practically at death's door."

"And I was being deputized to help you get dressed," Carla put in.

"Seeing that the rest of us are hardly eligible," Jim said, giving Lisa a disturbing glance. "I'm glad the patient survived."

"All my recovery is due to Dr. Shadrach's devoted care," she told him flippantly.

"Who's this Dr. Shadrach?" Carla asked.

"Family joke," Adam interposed smoothly. "More coffee?"

"No thanks." Carla folded her napkin and put it beside her plate. "I have to go down and take care of some final touches if we're going into town. Do I worry about a passport or anything?"

Adam shook his head. "A landing card's all that's needed. The purser's office will supply one before we go ashore. They keep your passport until you reach your final port of debarkation. We've already been cleared for Iskanderun; the Turkish immigration men came out in a launch and then took off again before we docked."

"Darn! I missed the whole thing," Lisa exclaimed. "I hadn't even noticed that we were tied up."

"Either that's a compliment to your companions," Adam began.

". . . or you spent so long getting dressed that you forgot to look out the porthole," James concluded.

"Don't answer that," Carla advised as she pushed her chair and stood up. "Please sit down," she instructed the two men, who were getting to their feet. "I'll be ready in about ten minutes," she told Adam. "Shall we meet at the gangway?"

"Fine. I'll look after your landing card."

"Good enough. See you later then. Have fun, you two," she told Jim and Lisa lightly and hurried out.

Lisa accepted a glass of orange juice from their waiter. "Nothing else, thanks. I'll have a roll from the basket," she indicated the wicker container in the center of the table, "and help myself to coffee."

"Why the preoccupied frown?" Jim wanted to know.

"Was I frowning? I didn't mean to. Actually, I was wondering how we could all go off and leave Rousch today. Not that I don't want to," she added hastily as she saw his expression start to stiffen, "but I thought that someone should be around."

"Actually, my dear, it's all been taken care of," Adam said. "We checked with Leon, the purser, last night and determined that no passports were being released today. Rousch would have the devil's own time trying to get out of the country in a hurry—the surface transportation from here is terrible and the Turkish authorities would certainly be annoyed to find anyone without proper credentials."

"In addition to which, both Rousch and Ceranini were partying last night." Jim extinguished his cigarette in an ash tray. "Rousch was poured into bed about eleven-thirty and the night steward assisted friend Sandro into his cabin near midnight. Ceranini was suffering from a swollen jaw at the time. Apparently he ran into a bulkhead," he finished blandly.

"Was he badly hurt?"

"Lord no. The steward dosed him with restorative brandy and a fine time was had by all." He bunched his napkin and put it on the table. "Hurry up with your coffee—our car's down on the pier now."

"That sounds opulent."

Adam chuckled. "You won't think so when you take a look at it. In Turkey, everything made in the 'States' comes in the category of a 'big American car' and they charge accordingly even if it's Stanley Steamer vintage. It's a good thing I know your intinerary and can come to the rescue if you get stranded."

"You make it sound like a dangerous mission," Lisa said, smiling.

"He certainly does." James was patently annoyed. "Maybe you'd rather I hired a horse and buggy, Adam. That way, we'd be sure to get back in time for the ship that calls in two weeks from now."

Thorson pretended to consider the idea. "It's a thought—but since I'm serving *in loco parentis*, you'd better stick to the car."

"I wasn't going to tell you," Lisa began, "but I did take a course in motor mechanics."

McAllister stood up. "Hell's fire!" he exploded, "when you two get through threshing this out, I'll be down on the dock."

Lisa watched him stride away and then turned to Adam, her glance curious. "You were a little hard on him. I wonder why?"

"So you tumbled to that, eh?" He pulled on his ear thoughtfully. "I've known Jim for a donkey's age and I'm very fond of him, but it doesn't hurt to put a few stumbling blocks in his way. Actually, it's the best thing in the world for these blokes who've had it easy."

"Easy in what way?"

"You could figure out the answer to that question. Jim breezed through law school and his bar exams. He has an excellent position with a respected Miami firm and a comfortable apartment efficiently run by a middle-aged housekeeper. Needless to say, she pampers him outrageously. To his credit, I'll admit his social life is not allowed to interfere with his career, but after a look at him, my dear, do you really imagine he has any problem finding a date?"

Lisa smiled ruefully. "Probably there's a blonde behind every palm tree and a brunette in the shrubbery by his front door."

"Exactly. And in Italy, his captain's daughter has spent most of her waking hours smoothing over any rough corners of navy life." Adam leaned back in his chair, jamming his hands in his blazer pockets. "Since you came aboard, I've seen Jim run through more honest emotions than I've noticed in years. Not all favorable, mind you. Apparently he can't decide whether to stand you on a pedestal or drown you. But at least he's having a thrash like normal people." His glance was kind. "I'm telling you all this to make sure you know the rules of the game. Knowing James, it's entirely possible that he'll decide the best course is to walk off the ship at the end of the trip without a backward glance. On the other hand," he said judiciously, "it could be up to you to administer a very badly needed coup de grâce. If you were the one to finish with a new scalp at your belt,

I think it would be the making of the man."

"So Operation Shadrach has other ramifications," Lisa said whimsically. "Did you plan this one, too?"

Thorson's smile was an admission. "The field of archaeology is a small one, and strawberry blondes stand out in people's minds. Let's say that your references were excellent—in all categories." He stood up. "I must be going or Carla will find another way to get into town and spend her money."

"Sure you're not flirting with a little bit of trouble there yourself, Professor?"

"Very probably," he nodded down at her benignly, "but I'm a downy old bird and the woman has too much sense to waste her time on such things."

"I wouldn't count on that."

"Don't fash yourself, lass." The lines deepened around the corners of his mouth. "That's what my Scottish friends would tell you."

She grinned up at him. "We'll see. Have a nice shopping trip."

"Thank you. You'll enjoy the crusaders' castle if Jim has recovered his temper by now. He's splendid company and utterly reliable. I hope the car he's hired is the same way."

"Don't give it another thought," she assured him, "I'll take along some chewing gum to patch the tubes."

"If you can smuggle a tire pump in your

113

purse, take that too." He gave her a genial wave and disappeared through the archway.

Lisa pulled her coffee cup closer and sat staring at the tablecloth. Adam's description of James McAllister's background was no surprise. That assurance of manner and action couldn't have developed any other way. It accounted for his decisive movements when Sandro proved obnoxious and for his equally decisive retreat whenever an emotion-charged moment occurred. She sighed and stirred her coffee absently. Undoubtedly he had been sidestepping anything to do with lasting emotions for years.

Despite the professor's enthusiasm for future skirmishes, she wasn't sure that she was eligible for the course. A very small exposure to James had proved as virulent as months of acquaintance with other males. She had no desire to be infected with a mammoth case of heartbreak, despite its benefits on the McAllister soul. Lisa Halliday's soul was extremely tender at the moment—about as tender as her shoulders, and in no condition for further exposure.

She took a final sip of coffee and stood up. Retreat was the order of the day, and for the rest of the trip as well. A cheerful retreat accompanied by determined friendliness that did not allow for any emotion. Shadrach would be dispatched back to his master's cabin and Sandro, if he ever sobered up, could be pressed into service as an ardent, if temporary, swain.

The sunburn that had felt so much improved earlier in the morning began to ache like a nagging tooth. Suddenly Lisa wished fervently that the entire trip was over and that she was on a plane bound for San Diego. She groped in her bag for a handkerchief. Depression was entirely normal after a bad case of sunburn, she assured herself, as she blew her nose vigorously and wiped her eyes. Depression—that's all it was.

It was a peculiar label for the six-foot specimen of American manhood who awaited her impatiently down on the pier.

CHAPTER SIX

Lisa settled back in the front seat of the vintage Dodge and watched green pastures of the Turkish countryside zip by.

"I can't imagine what Adam was fretting about," she said in a determinedly cheerful tone. "Aside from a loose spring poking me in an unmentionable spot now and then, this car isn't bad at all."

"Adam was fretting because ten years ago I got him stalled on the way to a dig and he's never let me forget it," James said with some amusement. "The old goat!"

"I like Adam."

"So do I," he retorted promptly. "He's as smart as they come with a fiendish sense of humor as well . . . so watch out." He pressed his foot harder on the accelerator. "I think this bus will hold together if we try it a little faster."

"Have we quite a way to go?"

"About twenty miles. It's hard-surface road all the way, so there shouldn't be any trouble if the engine holds out."

Lisa tilted her head. "I thought it sounded fine."

"It does now, but it wheezed pretty badly when I started it." He gave her a quick glance. "Don't worry, despite Adam's forecasts of woe, we'll make it back in plenty of time."

"I'm not worried," she assured him. "I'm sure you haven't any more desire to be stranded in Turkey than I have." She hurried on without giving him a chance to comment, "Although it looks almost like the countryside in the southwest or northern California—fenced pasture beside a paved road with a few billboards on it. It's a far cry from the bustle of Istanbul."

"You're not as far in the hinterland as it seems. There's a big American base fairly nearby and an oil pipeline as well. Both of them have given a tremendous boost to the economy around here."

"And they're the reason for the paved road?"

"Probably."

"Then I'm all for them." She returned the cheerful wave of a youngster who was straddling a fence post. "It's wonderfully peaceful, isn't it. There's hardly been any traffic so far, just an occasional truck."

"It's Sunday. Probably most of the people are sitting around in their villages."

"That always seems so strange in a Moslem country." She slouched down in the seat and let her head rest against the lumpy upholstery.

"Keeping the Christian day of rest?" He smiled. "They do the same thing all over the

117

world, no matter what the religion. Even in Singapore, you pay double time to the tailor if you want your suit finished on Sunday."

"I'll remember that," she assured him solemnly, "the next time I'm in Singapore. Since it *is* Sunday, do you suppose the castle will be crowded?"

He chuckled. "Where do you think you are, woman? This isn't Jones Beach or Brighton in August. At the moment, you and I comprise the only tour group. That's the advantage of a freighter." He reached forward and fiddled with the radio dial on the dashboard. "Want to hear the Turkish top ten?"

"All right," she said, relaxing. "It should be a great improvement when you can't understand the lyrics."

The twenty miles went by quickly to the accompaniment of discordant Turkish music. She closed her ears and ignored the tuneless parts.

James lowered their speed abruptly as they entered a small village comprised of a cluster of tiny houses and a solitary eating place. Men were seated outside at crude wooden restaurant tables while youngsters played by the corner of the building.

"This should be it," James said, turning left across the highway onto a dirt track. "Adam said the ruins were about a half mile down here."

She was amused at his preoccupied tone.

"You haven't been exactly forthcoming about what's in store."

Their progress slowed almost to a stop as the ancient car negotiated some of the deeper ruts.

"I thought you'd know more about it than I do," he said. "Don't forget, archaeology is just a hobby of mine, you're the expert in the field."

"Not over here. I was down in Mexico and Yucatan; all I know about the Mideast is strictly from hearsay. That's the main reason I came on this trip."

"You're different, anyway. Most women would still be complaining if they had to leave Paris for this." He nodded toward the somnolent countryside, broken only by an occasional hut set well back from the road.

"Stop lumping me with 'most women.' You make me feel like an uninteresting economy-sized package."

He snorted with sudden laughter. "Hardly, unless you gain pounds on our Italian diet."

"That's apt to happen."

He turned long enough to give her a swift, disconcerting glance and said, "I wouldn't bet on it," before concentrating once again on his driving. "Sorry about all the jouncing. Evidently the tourist bureau has a limited budget for road repairs."

"Nonexistent, I think," she said as an especially deep rut threw her against his shoulder. "Never mind. I'd rather have this than an eight-lane freeway and hordes of people." She peered through the windshield. "I think we're getting there. Isn't that part of a castle over there? And look . . . ," her voice rose excitedly, "there's a minaret among that group of buildings over to the right."

"Must be the local mosque. Adam said it was being restored." He let the car inch along. "We can pull off to the side here somewhere without any danger of causing a traffic jam."

"Heavens yes." She was gathering up her bag and her camera. "The only thing I've seen moving was that horsecart when we turned off the highway. You weren't fooling when you said we'd have it all to ourselves."

"Not quite to ourselves," he corrected, turning off the ignition and gesturing up the road. "The small fry are out even on Sunday."

Three little boys in the six- to eight-year-old bracket were grinning at them from the side of the road. Their white shirts, which had probably been immaculate several hours earlier, were grass-stained and rumpled. Stains were evident, as well, on the bare knees below their well-worn shorts. Their tanned feet were thrust into flimsy shoes tied on by a variety of laces. Each youngster carried a homemade but efficient-looking slingshot in his hand.

"Good grief," Lisa whispered. "Are we target for today?"

"There's one way to find out," James assured her cheerfully as he opened the door. "Hurry up, Madame, the tour group is leaving right now."

"Hey, wait for me." She got out and closed her door. "Since you're the guide, you can tell me where in the world we are."

"I don't think the village has a name, at least not on the road maps. They have such a wealth of ruins in this country they can afford to be casual." He took her elbow and helped her through the grass onto the rutted road. "Let's walk on this as far as we can. Adam said there's a path leading off."

Lisa found herself almost running to keep up with his strides. "You're going too fast," she protested finally. "Everything's been here a thousand years so it will keep a little longer."

He smiled down at her. "You've got it almost on the nose. These are ruins from the First Crusade. That building on the left was the forerunner of our modern motel, the rubble of stone straight ahead is the remnant of a small crusaders' castle, and the building standing off by itself is a villa built for Richard the Lion-Hearted."

She stopped abruptly, breathing hard. "And there isn't even a signpost to tell people about it."

James shrugged. "The natives know about it, so that's all that's necessary. Besides," he gestured toward the trio of youngsters following them at a discreet distance, "they furnish palace guards for the visitors."

Lisa took in the slingshots still clutched in grimy hands. "Guards my foot! If I know kids, they're doing a Turkish version of Daniel Boone being shadowed by the Indians. All they need are some trees to skulk behind." She moved on happily. "What's this about a medieval motel?"

He pulled her to a stop under a spacious stone arch and they peered into the shadowed gloom of a vast room. "According to Adam, this building was used by the caravaneers of the camel trains hundreds of years ago. From what he told me, there are remnants of kitchens, stables for the animals, public baths, and . . . ," he paused as if suddenly embarrassed and then continued lamely, "all the comforts of home."

Lisa's imagination quickly filled in the gaps of his description and she smothered a smile at his discomfiture. "Then let's tour the rest of it." Casting a quick look at the shadowed roof, she hedged, "Although I'm canceling out at the first sign of a bat."

"Don't be a nit. A bat wouldn't have a chance against the slingshots of our palace guard."

A good three hours later, Lisa called a halt.

"I give up," she said, having climbed to the top of a stone stairway in King Richard's villa. She slithered down onto a protruding ledge of the wide balcony overlooking the sea. Above them, carved stone arches looking like the moongates of Bermuda provided shade from the bright rays of the sun. Rubbing her ankles wearily she went on, "I know it isn't ladylike to complain that your feet hurt, so would it be all right to mention that each foot does—separately and in unison?"

James took off his sports coat and slung it carelessly over his shoulder as he looked down at her. "You did considerably better than I expected," he said with unconscious masculine superiority.

"Thanks a heap. That's one of the more dubious compliments I've received." She slipped a foot out of her shoe and waggled toes. "Sometimes I wonder how you ever got beyond the rank of ensign."

"I went in as a lieutenant," he told her dryly. "Most legal people do. How's the sunburn?"

"Fine thanks, so long as I stay in the shade. When we were up on that castle wall, I felt like a candidate for the barbecue pit."

"I was afraid of that. You and your inquiring mind! I hope to heaven you don't get a sunstroke because of it."

"The only parts of me suffering at the moment are the things called feet," she assured him, "and I haven't heard of any premature deaths caused by sagging arches. Besides, I wanted to see the thickness of those castle walls. Imagine, eight feet thick!"

"Reinforced by sections of basalt columns," he reminded her.

"Hundreds and hundreds of years ago," she mused, turning her head to stare out onto the calm greenish-blue water of the Mediterranean. "It's strange to think the men of the First Crusade were right here."

"Not too many of them made it this far. Thousands died of hunger and thirst before they reached this part of the *Via Dei*. The survivors were using goats and dogs to draw their loads when they got along here."

"Rough sledding for the 'way of God.'" A gentle breeze caught her hair and ruffled it. "Imagine building this villa for King Richard and then he didn't even stop overnight!"

"You can't blame the man, he decided to stop at Cyprus instead. Besides, that was a century later, so it wasn't a deliberate slight to the builders."

"You know what I mean. What a lot of work for nothing. This place is big enough to house ten families and it's remained vacant all through these years."

"I imagine most of the residents would prefer something with central heating."

"I give up!" She made a graphic gesture of dismay with her hands. "Here I am, submerged with the romance of this place and all you can think of is furnaces."

"Change that to food and I'll agree with you." He looked at his watch. "We're 'way past the lunch hour and well along toward afternoon tea by the *Lucarno* standards. Frankly I'm starved."

"All right, we can go." She slipped her shoe back on and stood up to peer cautiously over the edge of the embrasure. "Heavens, that's quite a drop."

He put a steadying hand at her elbow. "It's a good two stories and then some. Watch these stairs, the steps are uneven. Think what a shock King Richard would have gotten if he'd walked in his sleep."

She chuckled. "Especially if he strolled south instead of north."

"That's right. If he'd headed toward that archway . . ."

"Instead of toward the kitchen . . ."

"The whole course of history would have changed." James went on casually. "Had a good time today?"

"Marvelous! I want to take another picture before we leave, though. Let's see if we can get the palace guard against the villa for a crowd scene."

He pulled her to a stop halfway down the stairs and listened. There was the light slithering of footsteps behind them. "They're still with us. We'll put it to them in sign language outside."

"You shouldn't have any trouble after that slingshot contest you arranged," she assured him. "They'd do anything for you now."

Earlier in the afternoon, the gamin-faced

winner had happily accepted two packages of chewing gum as his trophy and now the boys were doing their best to chew through it as quickly as possible.

"I still have one package of gum left," Jim admitted, "so there's a chance for bribery."

"They're such sweet kids it probably won't be necessary," she said as they descended into the sunshine of the courtyard.

The palace guard followed them shyly, with smothered giggles, and Jim made the overtures to picture-taking. The three boys finally stopped laughing long enough to pose against the stone stairs, seeming disappointed when it was all over. They retired to perch on a broken wall nearby in order not to miss any further excitement.

"How about a picture of you?" James asked Lisa. "You'll want a reminder of Turkish sunshine when you're going through these slides on a cold winter night."

"We don't have cold winter nights in southern California," she said with a pertness that belied her desire to make the afternoon last as long as possible.

"In a pig's eye you don't." He reached for her camera. "Now if you lived in Miami, you could say that and mean it." He waved toward the arched doorway of the villa. "Stand over there. That way I can get some of the stonework for background."

"All right." She moved obediently to the building. "Is this where you want me?"

"Looks fine." He remained immobile for a minute and then lowered the camera. "Damn, this thing's jammed. The release button doesn't work."

Lisa frowned. "The safety must still be on." She started toward him. "I'll show you how to release it."

There was a sudden whoosh behind her and a thud jarred the earth under her feet. She shied like a skittish colt and whirled to see what had happened.

A watermelon-sized boulder had fallen in the spot where she had stood a moment before. "My lord," she whispered in horror.

"Get away from here." James was in front of her, kneeling to survey the jagged-edged rock. Stepping back, he shaded his eyes and peered upward. "He might still be there," he muttered and turned to enter the arched doorway.

"No!" For the life of her, Lisa couldn't have said whether her sharp cry of protest was premeditated. All she knew was that she simply could not permit James to disappear into that suddenly sinister recess. "Please don't go," she breathed, "I think I'm going to faint." She reached frantically for the wall's support as the ground heaved alarmingly upward.

James shored up her wavering form with a rocklike arm under her shoulders. "Come on," he said gruffly, bending down to scoop her up

127

against his chest, "let's get you in the shade." He strode over to deposit her on the ground beneath a gnarled olive tree. "Get your head down between your knees. Right now," he added firmly as she looked up in bewilderment. He put his hand behind her head and pushed to illustrate.

"Hey! That's enough," she protested thinly. "I don't bend that far."

"You're tougher than you think, my girl." The hand relaxed its pressure. "Feeling better?"

"Yes, thanks." She sat back slowly and was heartened to find that the countryside stayed right side up.

This time he guided her shoulders to rest against the tree trunk. "Lie against that for a minute and get your wind back." He flung himself down on the grass beside her and fumbled for a cigarette. There was a slight pause before he said casually, "I didn't think you were the fainting type."

A tinge of color spread over Lisa's pale cheeks. "I didn't think I was either, but I've never had such a close call." She managed a travesty of a laugh. "I've heard about death laying a finger on your shoulder, but not flinging boulders at your head. Do you suppose King Richard's ghost objected to our trespassing?"

"I'd guess this was a more contemporary haunt, but we'll never know."

"I honestly believe you're sorry that I kept you from going in and getting cracked over the head yourself."

"What makes you think I couldn't have done some cracking?" he replied as if stung.

She sat up abruptly. "Forgive me. I certainly won't interfere again. Your charming manner tempts me to do a little cracking of my own."

There was a shadow of a grin. "I'll ignore that because you're obviously suffering from shock. You were in the sun too long inspecting the castle." He took a final draw on his cigarette before extinguishing it carefully in the dirt. "What do you say about getting back to the car? I can provide a fireman's carry, clutch you to my manly chest, or manage a piggy-back ride. It's your choice."

"I can manage on my own, thanks." Not for worlds would she have let him know how attractive was the thought of being held securely in his arms again.

"Are you sure?" The banter was gone and he put a steadying hand at her elbow.

"Very sure." She took a deep breath. "Let's go."

They moved off slowly, Jim adjusting his stride to fit her shorter steps.

There was a silence for a few yards and then Lisa said, "That stone could have come from a weakened part of the roof structure."

"Umm ... possibly ... but I think you should stay out of dark corners for a few days."

"What about you?"

He took a deep breath as if struggling for control. "Stop fussing, will you? How in the deuce do you suppose I've survived all these years?"

"You needn't be insulting."

"I'm not being insulting. Frankly, I'm just madder than hell at this whole thing. And don't make any noises about being illogical. You realize that if the release mechanism hadn't jammed ... ," his voice trailed off and he sounded as if he were suddenly weary. "Honestly Lisa, save the worrying for your own neck or the younger generation like those kids this afternoon." His steps slowed and then stopped. "I wonder where they are?"

"They were watching when you were taking the picture. I don't remember what happened after that."

Simultaneously, they turned to look back at the villa.

The palace guard showed up plainly at the balcony on the upper story. Their game of stalking had evidently been abandoned in favor of charades. As Jim and Lisa stood transfixed, one of the boys leaned out precariously, aimed carefully, and then released a good-sized stone to fall onto the courtyard below. Lisa inhaled sharply as the dust spurted when the rock hit the ground. Above, the boys leaned out again to view the result.

"They must have seen—," she said in a voice that didn't sound like hers.

James's expression was set and forbidding. "Monkey see, monkey do," he quoted.

"Well, there's the proof you needed; no weakened roof structure after all. I should be sinking slowly in the west by now if something hadn't gone wrong with the plans."

He swore briefly, unintelligibly. "I don't care for your humor."

"It is pretty feeble, isn't it. I guess it's because I'm scared to death, James," she said simply. "It's awful to be declared expendable for a gold collar and two bracelets . . . even if they are XIIth Dynasty Egyptian."

"Stop talking like a female with the brain of a beetle and let's get out of here." He turned her around roughly and marched her up the path. "My interest in Turkish ruins just palled."

CHAPTER SEVEN

"You mean that gray jumble of buildings is Latakia?" Carla made a graphic and not too complimentary gesture. "All the guidebooks I read talked about the important city of the Crusades—not a mishmash of houses and streets covered with Syrian dust."

"Take it easy," Adam chided. "We're not even docked yet and you're writing off one of the most historically interesting cities in the world."

"Oh . . . professors!" Carla smiled indulgently. "The more dirt and ruins, the more romance. Isn't that right, Jim?"

McAllister, who was leaning against the rail watching the pre-docking activities of the crew, smiled briefly and agreed. "You have a point. I always thought it was a pity they couldn't fit in electricity and running water at the excavations."

"Plus a few dancing girls," Adam added sarcastically.

"Plus a few dancing girls. You don't have to be half dead to appreciate antiquity." He turned to Carla. "I never quite succeeded in getting this viewpoint across to Adam, however, so I can only wish you luck. There's always the nurse's office if you require some adrenaline for him."

"That's enough out of you, young man," Adam said severely. "Don't encourage her. After being dragged through every souk in Iskanderun looking for bargains yesterday, I could use that adrenaline."

"Where did you disappear to last night?" Carla asked Jim. "By the time we got back to the ship after dinner, everybody had vanished except Rousch and the Altoses. It will be a wonder if they don't run out of liquor aboard before we even get to Lebanon the way that threesome consume it."

"Were Rousch and the Altoses together?"

She shook her head. "No. Rousch was in solitary grandeur at one end of the bar and the Altoses were at the other. There wasn't any sign of Sandro, but the purser told us later that he was in his cabin nursing a stiff jaw. Apparently he ran into a door somewhere the night before."

Jim nodded regretfully. "You have to watch out for those doors every time." He turned to Adam. "I wonder what's causing the haze over that ship they're unloading at the end of the pier."

Adam raised his binoculars toward the freighter in question. "It looks like cement dust. I can't quite make out the name on the stern."

Carla, acknowledging Jim's change of subject only by the heightened color in her cheeks, brought the conversation back with a vengeance. "I don't suppose you'd know anything about Signor Ceranini's stiff jaw?"

McAllister favored her with a bland look. "Now why on earth would I know anything about that creep's state of health?"

"All right, forget that I asked. Adam said I wouldn't get any information out of you." She leaned over to brush an imaginary speck of dust from her black cotton skirt. "Is it any good asking what you've done with Lisa? There was no sign of her last night, either."

"She'll probably be up for breakfast. There's still about ten minutes before the gong."

"Eight minutes exactly," a light voice behind him corrected. Lisa, looking cool in a pale blue cotton shift, joined them at the rail. "I didn't know I was traveling with such a bunch of early birds."

"It only happens when I'm traveling," Carla confessed, moving over to make room for her. "I couldn't wait to get my first look at Syria."

Lisa looked at the nondescript port buildings of Latakia and she grimaced with disappointment. "I don't know whether I expected flying carpets, or what, but it isn't very exciting, is it?"

Adam clasped his forehead dramatically.

"God protect me from the female of the species! I wonder if Saladin's wives complained in the same way when he captured the city in 1188."

Carla looked slightly ruffled. "Well, I did expect more than a quiet port town. And certainly something more interesting than four Russian patrol ships at the neighboring dock." She gestured toward a pier just beyond their bow where the small naval craft were bobbing in the wake of the *Lucarno*'s tug.

"Be thankful we're being allowed to debark at the moment," Jim told her. "Americans were granted that privilege only in the last week or so. Il Supremo was telling me last night that Frau Witten and her son have to stay aboard today; Syria has never recognized the West German republic."

"I get the feeling that this isn't the place to do anything suspicious," Lisa said.

"Not if you want to sail with the *Lucarno* this afternoon," Adam agreed. "There's just about enough time to take a cab through the town and then make a short pilgrimage to Ugarit."

"Ugarit?" Carla said, pronouncing it carefully. "It sounds like something out of a tribal musical."

"Hardly, my dear. Ugarit was flourishing around 1400 to 1360 B.C. and has contributed greatly to our civilization," Adam said.

"Now you've really wounded him, Carla,"

Jim laughed. "Ignoring Ugarit in an archaeologist's company is like deciding to skip Mecca on a religious tour."

"She didn't know," Lisa put in defensively. "Most people have never heard of the place."

"You're certainly right about that," Carla said blithely. "It's easy to see I've been in the wrong company all this time."

"Not at all," Adam reassured her. "When I get in this part of the world, my own perspective slips a little. The thought of touring Phoenician ruins and seeing the birthplace of our alphabet makes me giddy."

Carla stared up at his rapt face and her expression changed to sudden understanding. "I hope you'll tell me about it," she said quietly. "Maybe it's not too late for me to learn something new."

His glance lingered. "Of course you must come along. We can make up a foursome today."

"Count me in," Lisa said quickly. "I've always wanted to see Ugarit. That is, if it's all right?" She raised her eyebrows at James.

"Why wouldn't it be?" Carla wanted to know.

"No reason that I can think of," McAllister drawled. "This is the time for both of you ladies to get educated."

"Aren't you coming along?" Carla asked.

"I'll have to wait and see. It depends on what I receive in the mail when we dock."

"There's plenty of time to make our plans later on," Adam assured them. "We can negotiate for a taxi when we want to leave."

"Negotiate in your fluent Syrian?" Carla asked skeptically.

"In my fluent French," he corrected. "They had a mandate in this part of the world until a few years ago."

Footsteps sounded on the deck behind them and they turned to see who was approaching. The Altoses were striding along hand in hand, apparently bent on a constitutional of sorts before breakfast. It was Mrs. Altose who pulled her husband to a stop.

"Good morning!" She greeted them in a high voice that saturated the entire side of the ship. "Isn't it a beautiful day! Simply gorgeous for sight-seeing."

Jim acted as spokesman in assuring her it was, thinking privately that of all manner of women the willow-slim bleached blondes with kittenish airs and plucked eyebrows enchanted him the least. Not that Max Altose was much better. His swarthy complexion was constantly set in lines of displeasure except on two occasions: when he was staring at his bride, as he was now, or when he was staring at his plate on the dinner table. Only then did the sullen expression disappear and a fatuous one take its place.

"Doesn't look like much, does it?" he was saying now staring at the nearby pier.

"Perhaps not from a cosmopolitan standpoint," Adam admitted, "but I am excited about visiting Ugarit. You must feel the same way; I understand you're something of an archaeologist yourself."

"I don't know where you got that idea," Altose said gruffly. "Stocks and bonds were my business until I retired. Archaeology's just a minor interest of mine."

"Why honey," his wife protested, "you know lots about all this stuff." She turned to Adam. "Last night, he was telling me about all the finds they've made at this place we're going today."

Altose's pudgy hand found his bride's and clasped it tightly. Lisa found herself wondering if it was as much affection as a warning, for he put in hastily, "Now baby, you'd better stop bragging. We're in with a couple of real experts here." He nodded toward Adam and Lisa. "Leon was telling me about you. I'm strictly a beginner at this archaeology stuff, but when I heard about the *Lucarno* stopping at all these ports I persuaded my wife that this was the ship for us. I've wanted to see these Mideast digs all my life."

The breakfast gong cut into the last of his sentence and an anticipatory gleam came into his eyes. "We'd better be getting along." He shifted his grip to his wife's elbow and quelled any further conversational attempts on her part with a glance. "The purser was going to try to get some breakfast melons for us in Turkey yesterday. I told him it was a damned outrage having to face that canned orange juice every morning."

"I don't suppose they can afford too many luxuries aboard a ship this size," Lisa demurred. "The passage fare was extremely reasonable and they've treated us very well."

"Makes no difference," Altose said snappily. "I told them they'd better get some decent entrees on the menu or the head office of the shipping line would hear from me." He favored her with a self-satisfied grimace that evidently was to pass as a smile. "You know what they say about the squeaky wheel—that's the one to get some attention. I'm not letting these fellows put anything over on me. Come, my dear," he turned his wife toward the door, "I believe in being prompt to all meals." It was a virtuous parting comment.

"That wife of his must have been out of her mind," Carla murmured as he disappeared through the heavy door.

"Or absolutely desperate for a husband," Lisa agreed.

"Mowrrr," James gave a creditable imitation of a cat's yowl.

"Don't try to shame us with that," Carla told him severely. "The man is a four-star pain in the neck."

"Who's shaming anybody? Frankly, I think they're evenly matched," he said calmly. "I can't work up any affection for either of them. At the risk of sounding just like him, though, I could do with a cup of coffee about now."

"I thought you'd never get around to mentioning it," Adam said with relief. "Let's go."

"You mean you aren't going to wait out here until the ship is safely docked?" Carla teased.

He waved a hand toward the longshoremen hurrying to place the *Lucarno*'s heavy lines over thick bollards. "I'll let Il Supremo ruin his breakfast with details like that. Remember the way he was expounding at the bridge table about the terrible dockers in some of these ports?"

"The only thing I remember about that bridge game was going down three, doubled and redoubled, on my four spade bid. There was no need for the captain to use that tone of voice to me, even though I couldn't understand his Italian. I hope you gave him my message that I'm giving up bridge for the duration of the trip and sticking to my needlepoint." She ran a hand through her wind-blown hair. "Do I look all right to appear in the dining room?"

"You look fine," Adam reassured her as he held open the door. "I meant to tell you about that message; it lost a little in my translation. It seemed easier to apologize and tell him you'd never make a bid like that again."

The door closed behind the pair cutting Carla's wail of protest in the middle.

"So much for her ultimatum," James told

Lisa. "What are we waiting out here for? We'll be covered with cement dust in another five minutes."

"Not unless the wind shifts. James . . . ," her voice trailed off.

"Now what's worrying you?"

"Max Altose, I guess."

"That character! He hasn't bothered you, has he?"

"Oh heavens no, not in that way. He doesn't know any woman is alive except that new wife of his."

"*New* wife? Where did you get that term?"

"From Sandro. Sandro Ceranini," she added unnecessarily. "When we were lunching the other day. He mentioned that Max Altose's new wife was a heck of a lot better looking than his other one."

"How did he know enough to compare?"

"That's the point I'm making," she said defensively. "Apparently Sandro met him a few years ago."

"In New York?"

She shook her head, causing the red tinge in her hair to glint in the morning sunshine. "No, not New York. Sandro said quite definitely that he met Altose in Beirut. He'd come into his agency there to arrange for a car and driver to take him to Bayt ad Din . . . the palace of Lebanese princes."

"He's sure of this?"

"Uh huh. He made a strong impression on

Sandro. While he was waiting for the clearance on the car, he was reading an Arabic newspaper—you know, all those squiggles and worms. Later, Sandro checked with the chauffeur Altose had hired. He confirmed that Altose was an old hand in this area, so that talk he was giving us was a lot of hokum."

"I'm surprised he'd try such a masquerade with Ceranini around."

She shrugged. "Maybe he thought Sandro didn't recognize him, or perhaps it was the other way around. Anyhow, he had no way of knowing that I was any more than a shipboard acquaintance of Sandro's."

"And are you?" Jim's tone was casual, but there was nothing casual about the set of his jaw.

"Heavens, not again!" She stepped back. "You know perfectly well what I meant. You can't spend half the trip snarling at me and the other half begging my pardon."

"I'm sorry," he began stiffly.

"See! There you go again."

"Oh for lord's sake, let's get some coffee. Didn't that foundation you work for ever tell you not to have discussions with a man before breakfast?"

"What a woman discusses with a man before breakfast was certainly not in the training manual."

"Then it should have been." He put up a hand and smoothed an errant strand of her hair. "Come on, let's feed the inner man and woman." Tugging open the door into the foyer he continued, "I find myself looking forward to the canned orange juice this morning."

"You are an optimist."

"Well, if it's a case of that or giving thanks for Altose's melons . . ."

"I know. We're stuck with canned orange juice for the duration." She looked over at him with a smile as they went through the dining salon archway saying, "At least, it's not Florida orange juice," and moved her hips sideways fast to escape the downward swipe of his chastening hand.

"Didn't your mother ever tell you not to strike a woman?" Carla asked as they joined her and Adam at the breakfast table. "Every European within sight will now go home and tell how they saw the rich American strike his woman."

"Correction please," Lisa put in calmly, "I'm not his woman and besides, he missed."

"If ever a man had provocation," James began.

"Premeditated too," Carla added.

"When I want a prejudiced witness, I'll know where to find one," he informed her with a grin. "What's the first course?"

"For us peasants, orange-colored juice," she said. "For squeaky-wheel Altose, a gorgeous Persian melon. I hope he gets indigestion."

"Tut-tut," Adam said reprovingly.

143

"Don't tut-tut me," Carla rounded on him severely. "You may have the disposition of an angel, but frankly Mr. Altose irritates me beyond measure."

"So drink your coffee and relax," Thorson told her. "You can always hope that he'll stumble going down the gangway."

"If you go about it right," Jim told her helpfully, "you could even persuade me to trip him. We are kindred souls on the question of Mr. Altose."

Carla beamed. "I knew you couldn't be all bad, even if you do beat women."

Lisa snapped her fingers. "There goes my staunch defender."

"Drink your orange juice," he advised, "you'll need your strength; Ceranini and Rousch have just come in."

"Are they on the shore party?" Carla asked.

"It looks like it. Rousch has socks on, and for him that's the equivalent of a black tie."

"How about Sandro?" Lisa didn't want to turn around and stare.

"He's wearing the usual," James informed her, "if you substitute black eye for black tie. You can add a nasty look directed toward me."

"I wonder why?" Carla asked innocently.

"Haven't the foggiest. Are you and Adam planning to hog all those rolls or are you going to share with your hungry shipmates?"

"Share away, friend." She passed the basket

to him while Adam filled coffee cups from the silver pot on the service table at his elbow.

"That's the spirit." Jim put a generous dollop of marmalade on his bread and butter plate. "Did Leon mention where the taxis would be available for Ugarit?" he asked Adam.

"Supposedly on the pier any time after breakfast. There's an English-speaking caretaker at Ugarit if we need any assistance out there."

"Do we flip to see who asks Rousch to join us?" Jim asked him.

The other looked resigned and finally nodded.

Carla's expression went rapidly from astonishment to suspicion. "You two are gluttons for punishment. I suppose there's an ulterior motive?"

Jim nodded.

"Maybe I'd better do the inviting." Lisa tried to keep her voice casual. "Better still, I'll ask Sandro if I can join their party. There's no use ruining things for the three of you."

"No." McAllister was emphatic.

"But why not? There shouldn't be any trouble with the two of them?"

"Give up, my dear," Adam said. "You can argue with Jim until doomsday and not budge him an inch. I'll do the honors and beg a ride with them." He held up his hand as Carla started to protest. "Don't forget, I have a perfect excuse."

"What's that?"

"I'll tell them that you two women plan to see the souks in Latakia and I want to get right out to the dig. Since I spent my time shopping in Iskanderun yesterday, there's no cause for Rousch to be suspicious."

"I think that has the earmarks of a nasty crack," Carla said.

"You're wrong," he assured her. "I had a splendid time yesterday. Jim will vouch that I don't go on shopping expeditions unless I want to." There was the shadow of a grin on his thin face. "All the same, feminine foibles make a perfect excuse for anything a man chooses to do."

"Or not to do."

He nodded and took a final swallow of coffee. "I'll go over now and put my proposition to Rousch."

"We'll see you out at the dig, then," Jim said.

"Yes indeed. I'm sure Rousch is as interested as I am in seeing it. The people at the British Museum said he had moments of being a fine archaeologist." Thorson pushed back his chair, favored them with a jerky nod, and strolled over to Rousch's table.

"It's all very well for Rousch, but I can't see Ceranini being fascinated with Phoenician ruins," Jim said.

Carla agreed with him. "Live strawberry blondes are more his hobby, I'll bet." Her teasing smile took any sting from her remark and she noted two suddenly lowered heads with interest. "No response from you, Jim?"

He transferred his gaze from the butter plate to her quizzical features. "I think strawberry blondes are a fine hobby myself."

"You're hopeless!" Carla retorted.

"Lisa will certainly agree with you on that."

Lisa tried to rouse herself to reply. Their conversation had brought back Adam's warning on Jim's customary behavior pattern. His words droned again in her ears. "It's entirely possible he'll merely abandon everything at the end of the trip without a backward glance." Everything and everybody. Only a fool would think otherwise. She bit hard on her lower lip.

The snap of fingers in front of her face brought her abruptly back to the present. "What are you doing?" she wanted to know as James leaned back again.

"Trying to get you back on the same plane with us. Evidently you could do with some more sleep. Sure you feel up to this jaunt today?"

"Of course." Her cool voice hid the turbulence of her racing thoughts. "I would like to take a short drive through town. If the idea of that puts you off, Carla and I could take a cab on our own."

"I can bear up under the strain of your company," he told her tersely. "It isn't every day I have such an enthusiastic invitation."

"Oh, help!" Carla pushed her chair back and stood up. "You two are off again. I refuse to referee, so you'd better declare a truce right now."

"Now you're being silly," Lisa said, standing beside her. "I'll be ready in ten minutes. Will you knock on my door when you're ready, please?" She thought of offering to return Shadrach in the interval but decided against it after risking a quick glance at James's stony expression. "See you later."

Ten minutes later Carla knocked and poked her head around the edge of the stateroom door. "Jim told me to tell you to bring a hat. Apparently, there's no shade out there."

"I have one." Lisa held up her packable straw with one hand and caught up her purse with the other. "Sunglasses, money, and shore pass—I think that's all." She followed Carla out in the corridor and carefully locked the stateroom door behind her. The free and easy security system of the ship changed drastically when they were in port.

Jim was waiting beside a ramshackle taxi parked by the foot of the gangway. He held the door open as they approached. "Come on, we're the last ones."

"Don't be so impatient," Carla told him as she followed Lisa into the dusty interior of the cab. "We didn't even stop on the way to look at the old coins and pieces of jewelry a man had spread out on the forward hatch cover. I hope he's there when we get back."

Jim got in and pulled the door shut behind him. "He'll be there. The shipboard vendors in these parts don't fold up shop until the very last minute before sailing."

The cab moved off in a series of jerks.

"Hadn't someone better tell him where we want to go?" Lisa asked from her corner.

"I took care of that before you arrived with the help of the ship's radio officer," James said. "We pooled our French, Syrian, and creative dramatics."

The cab drew to a stop by the main gate to the port and a uniformed guard waved them through after a careful look at their proffered shore passes.

McAllister sat back with a sigh. "We'll drive through town and look at the sights. Sing out if you want to stop anywhere. Otherwise, we end up at Ugarit. Okay?"

"Very much so," Carla murmured, busy with her camera. "Lisa, would you mind trading with me for a little while. I'd like to see if I can get any pictures through the window."

"No, stay where you are," Jim commanded. "I'll sit in the middle. C'mon Carla, up and over."

They managed the transfer without mishap, despite their driver's tendency to accelerate on the curves as if demonstrating that there was life in the old car yet.

"It's so quiet around here," Lisa said as they drove toward the center of town. "I suppose it's because there are so few automobiles on the roads."

He nodded. "You see it in all the underdeveloped countries—an emphasis on the cruder forms of transportation. Quite a shock after the traffic jams of France and Italy."

"It's even more pronounced here than it was in Iskanderun," Carla said. "There's no scarcity of donkeys though. Look at that one tethered on the corner with the huge pack on his back. I wonder if I can get anything worthwhile—," her voice trailed off as she raised her camera.

The driver, who was evidently keeping one eye on the rear seat, obligingly cut his speed and idled the engine until she took her picture.

Carla gave him an appreciative smile and settled back as the car sped forward again. "Adam said there wasn't much here. Not like Damascus."

"He's right," Jim agreed. "It's more straight subsistence-level living than anything else." He nodded toward a dingy market displaying pressed dates, oranges, cotton socks, and hardtack, jumbled together in untidy piles. "The local supermarket."

Carla stared at the long-skirted, black-shawled women who were elbowing their way toward the merchandise in much the same manner as their Western counterparts. "Evidently the shopkeepers do all right, even without television advertising. What do you think, Lisa? Is there any point in our joining the throng just to buy groceries?"

"I'm happy to see it from the car." She turned to James. "Have you noticed how new the mosques look, compared to most of the buildings?"

He nodded. "They must top the list of construction projects. It would be interesting to know who supplies the funds."

"Well, frankly, I'm disappointed at seeing all the public address speakers on the minarets," Carla said. "It must have been lots more thrilling when the muezzins were calling the people to prayer in person."

"But think of those poor muezzins shivering out in the cold light of dawn," he chided. "It's more comfortable to run a tape on the machine before you turn over and go back to sleep."

"There's absolutely no romance in your soul," she complained.

"Sure there is. I'm just looking at it from the muezzin's point of view."

She tilted her head to one side and gave him a speculative look. "Does anyone ever win an argument from you?"

"All the time. My bosses in the law firm would be pleased to supply all the evidence you need. Hey, that looks like a Roman ruin in front of us."

The driver was slowing the car so they could appreciate the ancient stone archway that had been preserved in a pocket-sized square. Neatly cut grass and surrounding green shrubs were an oasis of refreshment in the dusty block. Four barefoot children climbed happily on the few dilapidated park benches while their elders stood and gossiped. Two donkeys piled high with sticks were being urged along the cobbled street, disappearing into the narrow cavern of a native market.

"Do you want to get out and try the jewelry souks?" Jim asked.

"Not for me, thanks," Lisa said slowly. "The old man on the ship had some silver necklaces copied from those the Bedouins wear. I think I'll look at them when we get back instead. How about you, Carla?"

"I'll wait. It's too much of a struggle to plow through these crowded narrow streets. Besides," Carla fanned herself energetically with her envelope-type purse, "I'm about to wither away in this sun. Let's go on to Ugarit."

"Ugarit it is, then," Jim said, and got the directions across to their driver in shaky French embellished with graphic sign language, a maneuver climaxed by the Syrian's broad grin and a loud "Hokay."

The trip to Ugarit took only a half hour, despite an unscheduled stop for the driver to pick up a patched inner tube which he threw into the trunk with cheerful abandon.

"My God, I hope we don't have to use that," James breathed. "It wouldn't float a midget across a swimming pool."

"You don't have faith," Lisa told him. "What is it these people believe—'Insh' Allah,' isn't it?"

"What does that mean?" Carla asked.

"God's will," Jim translated, "but that inner tube would put one's faith to an insurmountable test."

All three heaved a collective sigh of relief when the car approached Ugarit safely.

"This is a rock-hound's paradise," Carla said as she gazed out on the acres of gray stone walls honeycombing the valley and hillsides. The never-ending pattern resembled an ancient maze, and only the fact that most of the walls were barely three feet in height kept it from being an impenetrable rabbit warren for unsuspecting visitors.

"There's so much to see, it's hard to know where we should start looking," Lisa said as they got out of the cab and left their driver settling down for a nap on the front seat. "Just imagine, all this is at least 3200 years old. It was a thriving city in Phoenician times."

"Don't get started on historical eras," Carla begged. "I can get mixed up on the Middle Ages and the Renaissance."

"Then Adam's the one to straighten you

out," Jim said. "He's great for putting it all in the simplest language."

"Do you suppose he's here yet?"

"I think so. There was another cab parked down the road a way. Let's go up here to the entrance and take another look for him and his friends." He steered the women up a rocky path toward a stone hut atop a small hill. The Syrian flag hung limply from an unpainted pole in front of the building.

"Don't go so fast," Carla panted. "It's a wonder the Phoenicians lasted as long as they did in this climate. There isn't a breath of wind."

"In those days, the sea came in this far," Lisa explained. "Look over there!" She stopped abruptly in the middle of the path and pointed to a rectangular stone with a square hole in the center propped up nearby. "It's a Phoenician sea anchor. Imagine! A marvelous thing like that just left out here on the hillside."

They walked on, more slowly this time.

Jim pulled out a handkerchief and mopped his forehead. "With all the trouble in the Mideast, the Syrians are more concerned about what's happening today than with their relics of the past."

"I wasn't going to mention those soldiers with the rifles slung on their backs on that hillside over there," Carla said nodding toward their left.

"A gun emplacement, I imagine," James said

calmly. "Don't worry, they're watching for invaders, not tourists."

"Those can be famous last words in the Mideast," she said wryly. "Let's check in officially so that we can collect our insurance benefits if the army gets nervous."

If the sentries were discouraging visitors, the man in charge of the official hut didn't mention it. He took their modest entry fee and assured them in broken English that the others from their ship were already surveying the ruins. If they took the main path from the cottage, they would encounter the royal tombs and the sacrificial stone to the great god Baal as the illustrated leaflet promised. His only warning was prompted by the watchdog in the enclosed run by the cottage. She had just whelped, he revealed, and was more apprehensive than usual, so if they would be sure not to tease or molest her in any way. . . .

Jim told him not to give it another thought and ushered Carla and Lisa toward the door.

Once outside, Carla pointed toward a flimsy-looking gate secured to the side of the building by a knotted rope. "The dog must be in there," she said. "I certainly don't intend to get any closer to find out for sure."

"I wouldn't," Lisa warned. "That gate doesn't look strong enough to contain a really determined guinea pig, let alone a big watchdog. Let's walk by very quietly."

The trio skirted the enclosure and tried to

ignore the menacing growl that told them their maneuver was not unobserved.

"I can see why this place isn't thronging with tourists," Carla said once they were safely out of range. "What with soldiers on the hillside and nervous watchdogs on the premises, I'm suddenly nostalgic for the Metropolitan Museum. Perhaps Rembrandt and Vermeer are more my speed than this." Her wave encompassed the rough-looking tufts of brown grass and weeds growing throughout the rocky field.

"You have to overlook the crudeness and try to envision the city as it once was," Lisa told her earnestly. She pointed to some ancient cisterns propped unevenly on stone bases. "There's a remnant of their highly developed water system."

James was perusing the leaflet. "Let's find one of the royal tombs, I want to see the stone work in it. Adam was telling me it was tremendously advanced for the period."

"They used a combination of seven," Lisa's voice rose in enthusiasm. "Seven stones to the entrance-way ... seven stones down to the crypt. ..."

"Help! I'm beyond my depth already," Carla moaned piteously as she surveyed their rapt faces. "Why seven?"

A masculine hail boomed over from a neighboring hillside, and they looked up to see Adam waving vigorously.

"You're being paged, Carla," Jim said with

some amusement. "It looks as if he's all alone. I wonder where Rousch and Ceranini got to?"

"It's not surprising you can't see them; you could lose an Elk's convention in this place. They're probably down on their hands and knees somewhere getting ready for the next descent to a tomb." She gave an answering wave. "I'll go and keep Adam company if you don't mind. Perhaps he can give me a quick five-minute explanation for all this before I dissolve into the gravel as a grease spot."

"Have a good time," Jim said absently but politely as she started down the hill. Then, "Lisa, we should take a look at the sacrificial altar first. According to this map, it's right in this area."

Carla was still smiling at their preoccupation with the past as she moved carefully along the rocky path toward Adam's waiting figure. "Hi stranger," she greeted him finally, breathing hard from her climb. "Jim and Lisa were so wrapped up in history that I felt like a ghost at the feast. Am I going to be a nuisance to you, as well?"

"Of course not." He pushed his disreputable straw hat over his forehead and massaged the back of his neck reflectively. "I hope I can condense all this and make it enjoyable for you. Archaeology may be the sacred grail for some of us, but I can understand why you wouldn't be interested."

"You don't have to bother with all the expla-

157

nations," she said baldly. "I really came out here just to be with you."

Adam stared down at her, an expression of astonishment on his usually serene face. "Did you really, Carla?" His voice was as uneven as an undergraduate's. Then his tone deepened. "It's very handsome of you to say that. Perhaps I should admit something as well. I've discovered that I'd rather have you tagging along for company than anybody I've ever known." He reached up and pushed his hat back so that he could look at her more directly. "I'm putting it very badly, my dear, but to be honest I haven't had any practice in saying things like this."

There was a moment of silence. Staring up at Adam's embarrassed face, Carla felt a burgeoning surge of affection; then her vibrant smile flashed to reassure him.

"You're doing very well indeed, Adam. So well that I'd like to cherish this feeling for a while. If that's being silly . . ." She hurried on as he started to interrupt, "No, I mean it. I didn't think it was possible to feel like this at my age. Let's continue the discussion later tonight on the boat deck. Who knows," there was the suspicion of tears in her laugh, "we might even give the Altoses some competition up there."

As if in a dream, she watched him slowly raise her hands to his lips so he could kiss the palms softly.

"Until tonight, then," he said quietly.

"Until tonight," she confirmed, feeling the pounding of her heartbeat in her ears. She pulled her hand away with an effort. "For a moment, Professor, I'll walk three steps behind you like Pocahontas. That way I can stand in your shade. Any historical tidbits you hurl over your shoulder will be greatly appreciated."

"Very well." The look in his eyes told her he knew very well why she was making this desperate bid for sanity in the middle of a sun-drenched Syrian field—or was it an Elysian field? He smiled gently and started off. "As I was saying, Pocahontas, the Phoenicians were an amazing people. Not only were they merchants but they invented the alphabet as well. The scribes living here separated and distinguished twenty-nine different simple sounds and designated them with a wedge-shaped script. Actually, the scholars at Byblos, where we'll be tomorrow, had made similar strides but their alphabet had only twenty-two signs. The Greeks adopted the Phoenician efforts and the alphabet went on to the Latins, eventually ending up in the West. But it started here 3200 years ago. Now what do you think of that?"

"Terrific, Professor Thorson! Tell me more."

It was amazing how pleasantly the time could pass, considering the discomfort of the surroundings and the soaring temperature.

Adam and Carla joined forces with James and Lisa at one juncture and then met the others from the ship outside the largest of the unearthed tombs. All differences were set aside for the moment as the hobbyists solemnly descended the seven steps to the underground recess so they could admire the magnificent stone fitting done by the masons thousands of years before.

Once on the surface again, Rousch stayed behind to compare technical notes with Adam while Carla and Mrs. Altose huddled momentarily under the shade of an olive tree.

Sandro, whose face was flushed under the brim of a jaunty straw hat, pulled Lisa aside as soon as she reached the top of the steps.

"Come with me, cara," he blurted out. "I thought I was never going to get a chance to talk with you."

Lisa's expression softened as she saw the obvious distress in his face. "I wasn't trying to avoid you, Sandro, but you can't blame me for being annoyed after your escapade the other night."

He groaned. "That's what I was afraid of. Will you believe me when I tell you that I scarcely remember any of my escapade, as you call it."

"That doesn't make it any better."

He fingered his bruised jaw ruefully. "Haven't I suffered enough? I have a good idea what kind of door I ran into." He glared over to where James was paying an undue amount of attention to the map in his hand.

"You were scarcely in condition to remember any details." She started to move away.

"Listen Lisa," he caught her arm, "there's a dance tonight in the lounge. It's the big event before we dock in Beirut tomorrow. Will you come with me?"

She disengaged herself gently, thinking that while she had no desire to foster their friendship, Sandro was a good safety valve for keeping things on a casual basis with James.

"No one has a partner for events on the *Lucarno*," she parried, "but I hope you will ask me to dance with you. I'd like that very much."

He gave her a smoldering glance. "Very well. That will do for the moment. I can see your watchdog approaching, so I'll round up Signor Rousch and go back to the car." He took off his straw hat and blotted the band with a handkerchief.

"Is the heat getting to you, Ceranini?" James's casual tone made it clear that he couldn't have cared less.

"It is hot, yes." Ceranini reached over abruptly and raised Lisa's fingertips to his lips. "Till tonight then, cara. Arrivederci!" He replaced his hat at a jaunty angle and strode off to where Adam and Rousch were still talking.

"Damnation." McAllister's look would have withered a lesser man on the spot. "What's he cooking up now?"

"Nothing very exciting. He wanted some

dances at the party tonight," she said, editing the truth slightly.

"I hope you asked if he was going on the wagon first?"

"It seemed better to leave things on an indefinite basis."

His look was cool. "That's one approach to the problem, I guess."

"Oh come on," she tugged at his arm impulsively. "Sandro isn't worth a fight. It's too hot."

"All right." He put a reassuring hand over hers. "I'll stop sniping. We'd better start back to the car."

They moved toward a rocky path that wound its way to the entrance.

"Are we going to be last?" Lisa wanted to know, giving a cursory look around.

"Adam and Carla are still by the tomb, I think." He shortened his stride to match hers. "Did you get the impression those two are enjoying life more than usual, or was I imagining things?"

"I was wondering, too." She pushed her hat brim back and stared up at him. "Wouldn't that be terrific!"

"A typical feminine reaction," he taunted.

"And what's a typical masculine one?"

He started to speak and then hesitated. "I thought we weren't going to fight this afternoon."

"That's certainly the coward's way out," she

said disapprovingly. "Are you going to put any obstacles in their path?"

"Try to dissuade Adam?" He chuckled deeply. "Surely you're kidding; he'd cut me down to size in no time. Besides, I think Carla's attendance at some of his faculty teas would liven things up no end."

She sighed with relief. "It's nice to think of something pleasant happening on this trip."

"I thought there were quite a few pleasant things emerging from it."

She let his remark pass unchallenged. "What I meant," she said carefully, "is that we're all suspicious of each other and it's getting more obvious all the time. Next thing you know, we'll need a program to keep track of who's running. We're trailing Rousch . . ."

"While Ceranini is never far away from you," he supplied.

She nodded. "And the Altoses are always somewhere in the background. Only Carla and the Wittens are completely in the clear."

"I'll go along with the Wittens. With their eating schedule, there isn't any time left over for games of spy and counterspy."

"Surely you can't suspect Carla?"

"Not of any dastardly deeds." He kicked a triangular-shaped stone toward the edge of the path. "I'm not completely satisfied with her appearance on the *Lucarno*. Let's face it, she'd be far more at home on a liner like the *Michelangelo* or the *Q. E. 2.*"

"They don't cruise these waters."

"I know," he said patiently. "But if you want a snappy Mediterranean cruise, you pick a ship calling at Dubrovnik or Corfu, not Iskanderun and Latakia. If you weren't interested in archaeology, you'd have to consult an atlas to tell your friends where in the deuce you were going. These towns are so small you can't even buy picture postcards."

Her silence acknowledged the truth of his statement.

"We know she isn't a buff on ruins," he added, pursuing the argument. "And having observed her wardrobe convinces me that the cheaper fare on freighters isn't the reason." He shook his head. "Frankly, I can't figure her out."

"Do you think she's spying on Adam?"

He looked amused. "If she is, then he's certainly enjoying the inquisition." Casually he pulled her hand up into the crook of his elbow. "I didn't ask for your identification, and that first outfit of yours was certainly a disguise. Sure you aren't a graduate of some Damascus spy school?"

"With red hair?" Her giggle was infectious. "I'd come closer to being a harem castoff. Thank goodness we're almost at the entrance hut. This heat has me huffing and puffing." She pushed back a strand of hair falling over her cheek. "Could we pick up a piece of this pottery on the ground for a souvenir? There are thousands of fragments strewn among the rocks and most of them are smashed so they could never be reassembled."

"I don't think anyone would mind. We can check with the old geezer at the building when we leave."

"Then I'm going to look for a piece with some significance—like the rounded lip of a water jug." She knelt down to examine a fragment by her foot. "This is like beachcombing, only better. Imagine how old these are!"

Bent over and intent on her search, she moved toward the kennel run by the stone building.

James looked up in time to see a flash of gray erupt from the back of the run and fling itself toward Lisa's stooped figure just beyond the flimsy gate. Sheer reflex action made him thrust his bulk between them as he shouted, "Get back, Lisa, for God's sake!"

Her startled scream came as the big dog's snarling form battered the barrier on one side and Jim wedged his weight against the other. Then, amidst frantic barking, the caretaker was suddenly beside them, calming the dog.

"James, are you all right?" Lisa ran her trembling hands across his chest as if to assure herself he was still in one piece. "Were you bitten anywhere?"

"It's just a scratch," he said tersely. "You head down to the car. I'll wait here until he gets her back in the doghouse and quieted down."

"I'm not leaving. You should have that bite checked as soon as possible." A frown creased her forehead as she stared down at his knee. "For just a scratch, your trouser leg is going to be quite a mess."

He merely grunted and then reached down to pick up a rope from the dust at the bottom of the gate. The knot was still intact, but the fibrous loop had been severed cleanly in the middle.

"Good lord," she whispered. "You mean that gate wasn't even secured?"

He nodded grimly and handed the rope over to the equally grim-faced caretaker, who started apologizing profusely.

"Skip it." James cut him off in the middle of a long sentence. He took Lisa's arm and marched her down the hill to the taxi. Halfway there, they met Carla and Adam coming up the path toward them.

"What's going on?" Thorson wanted to know. "We heard a scream and some shouting."

"Not much. I'll explain in the cab," McAllister said, shepherding them back in the direction of the car.

"Not much!" Lisa was still breathing hard from the encounter and their subsequent scramble down the hill. "That horrible dog bit him and he says not much."

166

"Simmer down and stop fussing. You can see for yourself that there was more damage done to my trouser than my knee. Thank God, the slats in that gate were so close that she couldn't get much of a grip." He pulled down a jump seat and sat facing them in the cab.

"Let's take a look," Adam said.

"Nuts," James told him succinctly. "Thanks just the same, but I'll live."

"You're darned tooting you will!" Lisa rounded on him fiercely. "When we get back to the ship, you're going to march down to the dispensary in double time. The purser told me there's an excellent nurse aboard, and she's the one who will decide if you need a doctor." Her pale cheeks suddenly became even whiter. "Lord, you don't suppose that dog could have been rabid."

"Hell no," James said. "She's the family pet."

"Some pet," Lisa said bitterly.

"I'm inclined to agree with you there." He stretched his leg out with an involuntary wince of pain as the driver made a sharp turn onto the main road. "However, it wasn't a four-legged creature who cut the rope holding the gate."

"What rope?" Adam asked.

Jim explained, and watched Thorson's face settle into grim lines as the obvious implication set in.

"So all four of us were sitting ducks as far as

167

that watchdog was concerned," McAllister concluded. "The rope couldn't have been off long or the dog would have been running loose and the caretaker would have seen her."

Adam nodded. "That leaves four other people with an opportunity to do it—the Altoses, Ceranini, and Rousch."

"You think this was done deliberately?" Carla was struggling to get a clearer picture in her mind. "What guarantee did they have that it would work? None of us said we were going back by the hut. As a matter of fact, Adam and I decided to take the lower path because it looked like a shortcut."

"If it didn't work, what did they have to lose?" Jim asked cynically. He cast a sharp glance at Lisa sitting quietly in the corner of the dusty seat. "Reaction setting in?"

She nodded slowly. "I haven't even thanked you for moving so fast. Another split second and the dog would have been through the gate and on top of me. I wouldn't have had a chance."

"Forget it. It's all over now."

"Is it?" Her lips twisted in a bitter smile. "I wonder." She took a deep breath. "I still think you're being a stubborn ape about your knee."

"Give up, Lisa," Adam told her calmly. "We'd overrule his decision and hold him down if it needed a tourniquet or something like that."

"I tell you, it's nothing but a scratch," Jim insisted.

"Well, you'll have a personal escort down to the nurse when we get aboard to find out if that's the truth," Thorson said. "Until then, we might as well change the subject." He reached over and opened Lisa's palm to remove the shard of pottery she was clutching. "Bless my soul, I think it's a piece of a water jug."

She stared at it distastefully. "I was going to ask the gatekeeper if it was all right to take it."

"Oh, I believe so," he said easily. "There were similar pieces over the whole hillside, so you haven't made off with a national treasure. Considering the antiquity, though, you have a nice little souvenir."

Lisa shuddered. "If you'd like it, please keep it." Her frightened glance went back to James's frowning face. "I have enough memories of Ugarit to last me forever."

CHAPTER EIGHT

That evening's festivities fizzled like a damp squib. Even the captain's dinner more nearly resembled a wake than the lively soirée promised by the bulletin board.

After a puzzled glance at his subdued passengers, the chief steward wondered if the fata morgana had suddenly deserted the turbulent Strait of Messina and moved eastward to spread its evil powers over the *Lucarno*. Unobtrusively he went into the bar and came back bearing a bottle of vodka. If caviar hors d'oeuvres weren't brightening the mood of his passengers, then reinforcements were needed. He removed the cork from the bottle and started making the rounds of the tables with his offering, carefully ignoring Albert Rousch, who ingenuously emptied the contents of his water goblet into a nearby bud vase so that he would have a good-sized receptacle for the free drink.

Once the passengers had eaten their way from antipasto to spumoni, they were summoned into the lounge for a command performance.

"Social life is taken very seriously on Italian

ships," Adam explained as he shepherded Lisa and Carla over to a settee, where a waiter hovered with after-dinner coffees.

"It certainly is." Carla glanced over to the end of the room where the captain, the executive officer, and the radio officer were sitting glumly on a divan looking like an unwilling court martial. "What on earth's bothering Il Supremo?"

"Anything that takes him away from his bridge game is automatically bad," Adam said.

"Don't tell me we're tagged for that again tonight?"

He shook his head reassuringly as he leaned forward to pour cream in his coffee. "I told Leon that we'd both had too much sun today."

"Good. Have you managed to escape the royal summons?" Carla asked Lisa.

The younger woman smiled faintly. "I told the purser that I can never remember what counts more, spades or clubs. That let me off the hook in a hurry. He knew Il Supremo would throw him overboard if he ever got me as a partner."

"And James takes great care not to be within reach when they're making up the nightly foursome," Adam chuckled. "It's unusual; he used to be quite keen on the game."

"At least, he had the perfect excuse tonight," Carla said. "You're sure they sent dinner down to him in his cabin?"

"Oh yes," Adam nodded, "though he didn't

feel much like eating it. He had a pretty rough series of tetanus shots from the nurse."

Lisa squared her shoulders. "I knew all along that bite was worse than he was letting on." She shivered. "I'll never forget the sight of that beast's jaws."

Adam patted her hand. "There's no use dwelling on it, my dear. I'm sure Jim isn't. Aside from feeling like a pin cushion at this stage of the game and finding it extremely uncomfortable to sit down, he isn't suffering any traumatic effects. Quite the contrary, in fact. He was looking forward to the next visit of the nurse when I saw him a little while ago."

Unaccountably, this didn't improve Lisa's mood. She took another sip of her coffee and shoved the cup away irritably.

Carla swallowed the last of hers and said, "I wonder if this brew gave birth to the expression 'nitty gritty.' I'd swear they put sand in with the coffee beans on this ship. You know, like gravel in with the bird seed."

"You've been aboard too long when you start criticizing the food," Adam told her.

"Well, it's either that or tear the passengers to pieces." She stared around the lounge. "We're back to our ethnic groups again. The Wittens are over in their corner."

"What's the boy eating?" Lisa asked.

"A handful of cookies that he snitched from the dining room. You won't find young B.B. unprepared. Mr. Rousch has now climbed on his favorite bar stool to be close to his source of supply." She let her gaze wander. "The Altoses have sorted a tremendous pile of records, so it looks as if the musical part of the evening is about to commence."

"I hope they turn the volume down on the phonograph," Adam grumbled. "The last time they played that thing you could have heard it in the North Sea."

The unnerving sound of a phonograph needle skittering across a spinning disc before it was put in a groove justified all Adam's forebodings. The sound blared out, filling the entire ship with a violent guitar and drum number.

"There goes Il Supremo," Carla said, not bothering to lower her voice because of the noise.

With a pained expression on his face, the captain moved majestically out of the lounge, stopping momentarily to execute a solemn bow in front of them. As the music continued to reverberate, he raised his eyebrows graphically before moving through the door.

The lesser officers, more relaxed now that their captain's august presence had been removed, settled down to shout at each other and cast appraising glances at the female passengers.

"Looks as if you two will have a couple of dancing partners in a minute," Adam rumbled.

"In that case, you'd better get in before the rush," Carla advised him.

Ceranini's voice sounded at Lisa's ear. "May I have the pleasure, cara?"

She glanced around in surprise. "Sandro! I wondered where you were. I thought you'd decided to give this a miss."

He pulled her to her feet and urged her toward the small dance floor. "Hardly. Not after our talk out at the ruin." His arms enclosed her tightly. "This is what I've been thinking about."

She tried to pull back. "You don't hold your partner so closely with this kind of music."

"Then they can change the music. I'm not going to stand by myself snapping my fingers and—how do you call it—gyrating, when I can be holding you."

She pulled back again, breathlessly. "That's all very well, but there's no use attracting attention."

"Who's looking at us? Anybody dancing has enough to do trying to stay upright. I think we're hitting some offshore swells." He carefully swung her in a slow turn in order not to lose balance on the tilting floor. "Your friend Carla has been partnered by the executive officer. Is that why Professor Thorson is looking so unhappy by himself?"

"He's not looking unhappy; he's just observing." Adam's arm was draped along the top of the divan and he was absently beating time with a book of matches. She brought her glance back to the dance floor. "Who's the nice-looking blonde in white?"

"Leon's partner? That's Maria, the *Lucarno's* nurse. She's fond of dancing and he must have persuaded her to slip away from her duties for a few minutes."

"You seem very familiar with all that's going on," she commented dryly.

He shrugged. "It's a small ship. Dio! The radio officer has asked Frau Witten to dance. He looks like a tug pushing a battleship around."

She looked over her shoulder to see the red-cheeked woman beaming down on her slight partner. "I suppose she gets tired of just sitting on the sidelines with her son."

"The crew won't let her be unhappy. Leon will take his turn and then some of the rest. That's what they get paid for."

"Leon is as red in the face as Frau Witten."

"That's because he caught too much sun this afternoon on his time off." He kept his hand at her waist as the record finally ended.

"Hadn't we better sit down?"

"And let the vultures have a chance?" His arm tightened protectively. "No, we will wait here. The music will soon start again." There was a scratchy needle sound before melody once again filled the room. "Ah, this is more my type." He pulled her close and they moved off in a languorous fox trot. "How did you es-

175

cape McAllister tonight? I thought we would be trading insults by now."

Surprise made her stop in the middle of the floor. Then she yielded to the pressure of his hand at her waist and they moved off again. "Didn't you know? He had to go through an entire series of tetanus shots because of that miserable dog bite at Ugarit."

It was Sandro's turn to falter. "No, I hadn't heard."

"Strange that Leon didn't tell you, or your friend Maria. I thought everybody aboard ship knew about it."

"A nurse doesn't discuss her patients," he said somewhat stiffly, "and Italian ship's officers don't discuss the passengers."

Her lips twitched. "At least, not with the other passengers." She acknowledged his glare. "All right Sandro, I'll stop teasing, but Italians have their minor vices too."

He shook with sudden laughter as he touched his bruised jaw. "You should know, cara. For the moment, I forgot."

The fleeting glimpse of the Sandro she had once known made Lisa feel more cheerful. Perhaps the attacks she and James had endured were merely quirks of fate, after all. Then her mind went back to the scene of the Turkish boys acting out their grim charade and the severed rope lying in the Ugarit dust. She shuddered so violently that Sandro tightened his hold in concern.

"Lisa, what is it? Aren't you feeling well?"

"I'm fine, Sandro," she reassured him automatically. Surely his amazed expression when he heard of James's accident had been genuine, so there was no need to be suspicious of him. But if Sandro wasn't involved, Albert Rousch or the Altoses were.

A formidable bulk caromed into Lisa; only Ceranini's deft maneuvering saved her from falling flat on her face.

"Scusi, scusi, Fraulein." Frau Witten, still in the arms of her perspiring partner, gave her a beaming smile before towing her escort like an unwilling burro back into the dance.

"Are you all right, Lisa? That terrible woman— I could not move out of her way fast enough. She advances like an armored division and takes up the entire floor." He mopped his brow. "Let's go out on deck and catch our breath for a few minutes."

Lisa was smitten with indecision. It would be wonderful to go out and get some fresh air. On the other hand, she was sure that Adam and James would be strongly opposed to any lonely strolls on the open deck. For that matter, she wasn't sure enough of Sandro's innocence to welcome them on her own accord. Motion picture films of tremulous heroines strolling into dark caverns and deserted houses always made her feel the stupid females were deserving of whatever the next reel had in store.

Perhaps she could ask Adam. Where was Adam anyway?

At that moment, he was politely but firmly cutting in on the officer who was twirling Carla in a modified Naples stomp over the foyer floor. *"Scusi signore,"* he said genially, moving Carla safely out of range. "My dance, I think. Canadian *passeggero,* you know," and danced away before the amazed Italian could speak.

"Thank heavens," Carla said, settling happily into his arms. "I thought I was going to break in two before the record finished." She chuckled. "Your Italian is magnificent. Next time you must try using some verbs."

"Don't be fresh, young woman. You'll note that I accomplished my objective."

They danced contentedly for a few minutes.

"Ummm, this is nice," she said dreamily. "You do a mean fox trot, Professor. Are you as good at other things?"

"I daresay I can improve with practice. Strange things are happening already. Imagine me, at my age, making assignations for the boat deck."

"It's very becoming. All my life, I've hoped that some attractive man would invite me for a moonlight stroll on a boat deck."

"From now on, anyone else who issues an invitation like that gets a severe talking to."

"Adam, you do wonders for a woman's morale. At the moment, I don't feel a bit like a tired magazine writer on the terrible side of forty. I think I'd better stay out of the moonlight and have a cup of coffee until I come back to my senses."

"The hell with coffee, we'll have champagne," he said masterfully. "And we have to stay out of the moonlight for a while, I promised Jim I'd keep an eye on Lisa tonight."

"After what happened this afternoon, I think that's a very good idea." She patted his shoulder consolingly. "Don't worry, the moonlight will keep. We'll ask Lisa to join us in a glass of champagne. She could do with cheering up."

"All right. I suppose we'd better include Ceranini in the invitation."

"You might as well; I think he intends to stick as close to her as possible now that Jim is out of sight."

He walked her back into the lounge and glanced about. "Damn!" he said softly. "Jim will have my head. She's disappeared."

Lisa wasn't far away. Just then, she was leaning on the railing at the after part of the promenade deck. Any accidents in that part of the ship could only involve a six-foot fall onto the freight deck below. In the event of such a remote possibility, the roof of the tiny Fiat secured on the deck underneath would suffer far greater damage than she would.

"Are you sure you want to stand here?" Sandro inquired anxiously. "The breeze is stronger at the bow."

"But the view is lovely here," she insisted.

He stared down at the deck cargo chained to rusty deck plating and then at the darkness beyond. "Well, if you say so." His manner indicated that her taste was abominable but he was willing to go along with the idiocy.

"Absolutely marvelous," she pursued blithely. "Just breathe that air." She took a deep breath as she spoke and discovered that they were standing directly under the exhaust fan from the galley. Somewhere inside, someone had been frying fish.

Sandro sniffed dubiously, but beamed and shrugged his shoulders. His thought was that of a man who has just pushed a lead slug into the slot machine and hit a twenty-dollar jackpot. Obviously, Lisa was easier to please than he had remembered. Perhaps the furor about spoiled American women was just newspaper propaganda after all. He edged closer. "You have forgiven me then, for my behavior the other night." His arm moved slowly up to her shoulders. "My beautiful Lisa, what wonderful luck to find you aboard. I can't wait to show you Beirut." Deftly he raised her chin with his other hand and covered her lips with his.

Damn, oh damn, Lisa thought as she stood quietly in his tight embrace, what do I say now? I can't tell the man that he simply leaves me numb, not a handsome creature like Sandro.

Then she pushed hard against his chest. "Don't Sandro, that's enough."

His arms fell reluctantly. "What's the matter?"

"I'm not sure," she faltered. "Please forgive me, I'm not feeling well tonight. I think I had too much sun this afternoon."

He was obviously disappointed at such a feeble excuse but tried not to show it. "Of course, Lisa. This climate takes some getting used to. You'll appreciate the coastal breezes in Lebanon, it's a much healthier country. You must let me show you some of the beauty spots around Beirut."

"How kind of you, Sandro! But I have to wait and see what plans Carla has made." She deliberately avoided any reference to Adam or James.

"I'm surprised at your choice of companions, my dear." His tone was reproachful. "With Miss Broome's background, I don't believe she is the ideal friend for a woman your age."

"That sounds mid-Victorian. What on earth do you mean?"

"Haven't you seen the kind of writing she does for that scandal magazine? Articles like 'What Aging French Millionaire is Dating what Italian Starlet?' That sort of rot. I think her latest had to do with an American socialite who was involved in an English drug-smuggling ring. All in very bad taste."

"If it was so terrible, why did you read it?"

He moved back as if she'd struck him. "That has nothing to do with whether she is the proper companion for you."

"You're taking it too seriously." She soothed him, recognizing the typical attitude of a European male. "We're merely two American women who happen to be on the same ship. It doesn't matter how Carla earns her living so long as it's honest. At the moment, she's on a vacation."

He shook his head. "You're wrong about that, too. Miss Broome is very much on the job."

"Now you've lost me completely. What job are you talking about?"

For the first time, he looked ill at ease. "Perhaps I shouldn't have mentioned it."

"Perhaps not, but you have and you can't leave me dangling."

"Not if I'm to have any peace, eh? Very well. I'm not too sure of the facts, but there's a rumor going around Beirut that some stolen jewelry is to be moved."

Lisa drew in her breath sharply. "You're not accusing Carla of being a jewel thief?"

He made an impatient gesture. "I didn't imply anything of the sort. With her job, she's probably waiting to see if there's going to be a story in it."

"If this is common knowledge, the Lebanese police must be waiting too."

"I didn't say it was common knowledge, Lisa.

182

It would be safer to say it was very uncommon knowledge." He gave her a quelling look. "Safer for you, cara, if you forget this entire conversation."

She moved back a step. "Consider it forgotten," she said airily. "I've heard about Middle East intrigues before, and I have no desire to get mixed up in one. You'll have to excuse me now, Sandro. I'm getting a rotten headache."

Immediately he was all solicitude, bending down to press a gentle kiss on her cheek. "Of course, my dear. Let me walk you to your cabin."

"It isn't necessary."

"But I want to," he insisted, moving along the deserted deck beside her.

And I would much rather be alone, she was thinking nervously. It was a terrible strain to look nonchalant when in reality the slightest untoward move he might make would send her screaming for help.

A door opened amidships and the sudden appearance of the dapper little purser made Lisa feel like shouting for joy.

"*Buona sera, signorina,*" he greeted her cheerfully. "I am looking for a dancing partner. If your escort didn't make two of me, I would challenge him to a duel. He had no right to steal such a beautiful passenger."

"Too bad, Leon, but you'll have to keep searching," Sandro said. "Signorina Halliday has a bad head and is going to her cabin."

183

Leon clasped his brow theatrically. "I refuse to go back in there and dance with Frau Witten one more time. Sandro, you should be shot."

Lisa stepped inside the door that Sandro was holding. "It's too late for a duel tonight. Why don't you make him buy you a drink instead?"

"But a very quick one," Leon specified. "If the captain sees me sitting at the bar, I'll be yanked into a bridge game. He's still hunting for a fourth."

His warning was all that was needed.

"In that case, we will move rapidly," Sandro decided. He raised Lisa's fingers to his lips and said, "*À domani*, cara. Tomorrow, I hope you feel much better."

"Thank you." She eased her hand away. "Good night, Leon."

"*Buona sera, signorina.*" His good-natured face crinkled in a smile. "If I am caught by you-know-who, I think I'll have a bad head, too. Perhaps it is catching." One eye closed in a droll wink.

She grinned and went down the winding stairs to the stateroom deck. As she moved into the corridor, a noise on the opposite side of the ship caught her attention. Her heartbeat accelerated as she saw a familiar tall figure disappearing into his cabin. So James was up and around. She walked slowly on and opened her stateroom door. It was strange he hadn't come up to the lounge if he was feeling well enough to be dressed and wandering on the lower decks.

She walked over to her dressing table and put her purse down on the top of it. Then, still moving slowly, she picked up the glass camel from his place of honor in front of the mirror. She stared down at him calculatingly as she ran a caressing finger over his bowed neck. "What do you think, Shadrach? Under the circumstances, is it proper to pay a sick call?" Her finger flicked the end of his nose impudently. "The heck with the circumstances, let's go."

James took his time answering her knock on his stateroom door. He was still fully dressed, but his tousled hair looked as if he had been raking his fingers through it. "This is a surprise," he said coolly, making no move to let her in. "It's a little late for visiting hours, isn't it?"

His unfriendly reception bewildered Lisa, but she managed a faint smile. "I didn't realize you were such a stickler for convention. Besides, I brought along a chaperon."

An answering grin played over his face as he accepted the proffered camel. "So Shadrach's playing duenna. In that case, you'd better come in."

She noted that he left the door ajar behind them. "I'm sorry to have disturbed you. Actually, I wouldn't have intruded if I hadn't caught a glimpse of you when I came down to my cabin just now."

He glanced at his watch. "Festivities all over, or is this just intermission for you?"

She flushed at his tone but kept her voice level. "The dance didn't amount to much. I was planning to stay down. Since your camel was pining away in my cabin, I thought he might as well keep you company. How's your invalid state, by the way?"

"I'm fine, thanks. Just don't ask me to sit down. That tetanus series is worse than a day of bronc busting." He measured the stateroom with a considering glance and then removed a pile of books from the chair at the end of the bed. "Make yourself comfortable."

"Thank you." She perched uneasily on the edge. "This furniture leaves a little to be desired, doesn't it?"

"Maybe. But I know damned well that Emily Post wouldn't approve of your sitting on the bed."

"I wasn't suggesting— oh never mind." Her voice trailed off but she gave him a defiant look. "Would it be any use asking why I'm in the dog house this time? You really should put up a sign, like one of those that says the dentist is in or out. That way, I'd know what to expect."

"You're a great one to talk!"

"What is that scintillating remark supposed to mean?"

"Just that it might be a good idea if you wore a sign too. Then you could keep track of the man in your life at the moment. When I went up to the lounge, I found Adam in a tizzy because you'd disappeared. I went searching through all the dark corners on the ship, expecting to find your broken neck in one of them. Instead, I come upon it being fondled by your favorite pseudo-Lebanese muscleman." His words came out like ice chips. "If you can still remember what happened earlier in the afternoon you'll recall there was a damned good reason to think he could have been selecting you for dog food." He watched her stand abruptly and hang onto the back of the chair for support. "I know women need some love interest in their lives," he continued cruelly, "but if you're that hard up, I think you'd better see a psychiatrist when you get home or look for a steady boyfriend."

Lisa's eyes blazed at his accusation. She moved over to his lounging form and deliberately slapped him as hard as she could manage. Then she turned and bolted for the doorway.

"Oh no, you don't!" James caught her by the wrist as she reached the corridor. "You want to play rough, we'll play rough." With his other hand, he reached into her flowing hair and yanked it hard, forcing her face up to his. He ignored her struggles and edged her body into the niche between the door and the corridor walls so that she couldn't escape. Then, purposely taking his time, he crushed her parted lips under his.

Neither one could have told how much time passed or just when the kiss changed from a violent struggle for supremacy into a passionate embrace that kept them clinging together. The sound of a noisy giggle forced them reluctantly apart.

With dazed looks, they saw young Master Witten scamper down the last part of the stairway and beat a retreat to his cabin, still giggling at their discomfiture.

James muttered something profane under his breath.

Lisa pushed away from him, scarcely conscious of how her hands had come to be circling his neck.

"Did you have fun?" Her voice was bitter with humiliation. "From now on, I'll take my chances with Sandro rather than an oaf like you."

The insult had no tangible result. He leaned against the doorway, breathing more quickly than usual but otherwise back to his determined and assertive manner. "You won't have to worry again. Go down and write in your diary that you had a successful evening." The glance at his watch was obvious. "After all, it's fairly early; you might still find green fields if you visit the lounge later on. But don't try to slap me again," he warned, as she straightened indignantly, "or you'll find yourself in a situation where even young Witten can't save you."

"Don't you dare touch me—," she managed, with tears of anger in her eyes.

"Relax, Miss Halliday." He moved back into his stateroom. "I've got better things to do."

The door slammed behind him and there was the insulting sound of a key turning noisily in the lock.

CHAPTER NINE

Never let it be said that an archaeologist from California can't feign casual indifference as well as a Florida lawyer, any season of the year.

The sudden dissension in the ranks became obvious to Carla and Adam at breakfast the next day. It became even more obvious when Lisa appeared and announced to a spot six inches above James's head that she was breakfasting at Sandro's table by invitation, so if they would excuse her. . . .

"Now what's eating her?" Carla asked, as they watched Lisa head across the floor. She fixed an accusing glance on the younger man. "What did you do to her last night?"

"Notice that, Adam?" McAllister replied, unperturbed. "How the female of the species goes immediately to the attack, justified or not."

"The one thing I *have* noticed during a long, if unproductive, life is to avoid conversations like this at the breakfast table."

A reluctant grin passed over Jim's stern features. "You're even smarter than I gave you credit for, my friend. See that you make a note of his rule for the future," he said, turning to Carla.

"I will—but how did you know about us?" She stared at him in amazement. "We thought we were keeping things dark."

"Dark and still, we inly glow," he quoted. "I'm only surprised Adam was able to hold out this long. There'll be a great ringing of the bells when you get him back to Canadian shores. Females have been trying to snare him for years."

"Certainly. Elusive Thorson, they used to call me. At least, I seem to have been more successful in my courting than you."

A dull red covered McAllister's cheeks. "Who's courting? I thought we'd agreed to change the subject."

"We didn't, you know, but never mind," Carla said. "I'll get the details from Lisa later on." She cast an amused glance over at the table against the wall. "Providing I can pry her away from Sandro."

"Why waste your time." Jim pushed away his empty coffee cup as if it offended him.

Carla peered over into it like an inquisitive bird. "I wonder if you can read coffee grounds the way you do tea leaves?"

"Behave yourself," Adam reproved. "We should be in Beirut in another hour. How do you think we should work things here, Jim?"

"I wish to God I knew. Obviously, we can't

follow everyone on the passenger list. After yesterday's action, we might as well continue to concentrate on the Altoses, Rousch, and Ceranini. If you and Carla attach yourselves to the Altoses, I'll follow Rousch around, and it shouldn't be any hardship for Lisa to tag along after Ceranini."

Thorson nodded. "We'll probably all visit the same places." He scratched the side of his nose reflectively. "Except for Ceranini. He might have a different list since he lives there."

"What's on the tour schedule today?" James asked.

Carla consulted a brochure by her plate. "They've planned an afternoon shore excursion to Byblos. Tonight, they're making up a party to see the naked women at the famed Casino du Liban."

"Does the booklet say that?" Adam asked incredulously.

"Not in so many words," she admitted. "I was talking to the steward earlier. Apparently the Beirut casino is more sensational than the Strip at Las Vegas and the Lido in Paris put together. Can we go?"

"Say yes, Adam," Jim instructed. "I was talking to the steward, too. If you get tired of looking at the stage show, you can always gamble away next year's salary."

"Dispense with the sales talk," Adam said austerely. "I went to the casino on my last trip."

Carla gave him a dark look. "Hah! I might have known."

"A project of pure research," he assured her. "Let's take things as they come and attach ourselves to the Altoses."

She shrugged. "That might have its brighter moments. Mrs. Altose has been panting for a chance to see the jewelry souks in Beirut."

"And you'll lend yourself for the sacrifice and go along." He grinned and leaned back in his chair. "You're both going to be surprised; there are jewelry stores here to rival Tiffany's. Beirut is the place where all the rich sheiks come for their relaxation. There are luxury hotels and shops to equal anything in Europe. The Lebanese are called the Swiss of the Mid-East."

"No more dust and romance?" Carla wailed.

"Not much. The Beirut tourist password is 'Bring money,' the natives do the rest." His tone was reminiscent. "Food at some of the hotels is magnificent. That's not surprising, when you remember the country was under French control for many years. They left a splendid legacy in wining and dining. The only illness most visitors suffer is writer's cramp brought on by signing too many travelers' checks. Now that business is slowed by the Israeli conflict so nearby, the prices on silks and jewelry are supposed to be better than ever."

Carla smiled at him proudly. "There's nothing like an educated man who uses all that knowledge for practical things."

"You can certainly go shopping, my dear, but you must visit Byblos, as well. After all, how often are you next door to the earth's oldest inhabited city?"

"Darling, you're a past master at the soft sell. I'll be delighted to wear my ankles down looking at Byblos."

"I'll leave you to it, then," Jim said, putting his napkin on the table and getting up. "We can meet on deck later. Best wishes again, Carla. Put your mind to organizing an engagement party."

"I will," she promised solemnly, "right after I get Adam to take me to the casino. Pure research for my magazine."

Thorson groaned as he pushed back his chair. "It looks as if I'm caught in a web. Excuse me, you conniving woman, while I have a few words with Jim. I'll be back in a minute."

"Of course. See you later."

The two men strolled into the deserted foyer where Adam took a quick look around before asking, "Are you following the original plan and meeting your contact this morning?"

The other nodded. "He should be coming aboard with the pilot and immigration officials any time now. That's why I want to get down to my cabin."

Adam chewed irritably on his lower lip. "I don't like this isolation. We can't very well use the ship-to-shore phone they'll be connecting at the pier, and any other communication is apt to be blocks away in the dock area. It's going to be damned difficult keeping an eye on these people."

"Ancient oriental proverb says, never try to catch two frogs with one hand."

"Very funny."

"Stop acting so glum, Professor. I think the whole idea is impossible too. It would be merest luck if we caught Rousch or his confederates with the treasure."

"The authorities know that. Actually, we were never expected to do more than hold a watching brief. The incidents at Iskanderun and Ugarit show that the people involved are reacting to the pressure."

"Reacting isn't exactly the word I would have chosen," Jim said dryly. "I wonder if we'll be as lucky on the next go 'round."

"Don't forget that in Lebanon we're supposed to have some help. The British and American embassies are organizing joint surveillance. They feel Beirut is the key port for Rousch."

McAllister nodded. "It's the obvious place for him to collect the stuff and the one place he could manage a quick flight to Cairo. Lord, I'll bet the Lebanese will be glad when we sail away. Betwen the Israelis and the Arabs, they have enough secret agents in Beirut now to make it like Lisbon during World War II. We'll have to wear lapel badges so they can tell who's following whom."

"Laugh if you like," Thorson told him grimly, "but don't go getting yourself shot. Other than collecting on your life insurance there won't be any other benefits. These days, we're as welcome to the Lebanese authorities as an outbreak of plague. The ground rules are that we can do all the gumshoeing we want but they will not get involved."

"In other words, hide your bodies under the rug and don't whistle for a policeman."

"Exactly."

"I'll be sure to remember. Are you going to tell our Miss Halliday about all this?"

"She knows as much as I do."

"The blind leading the blind, eh? Okay, I'm going down to my cabin."

"I didn't mean to discourage you."

"You didn't. Only admirals look happy; lieutenants just follow orders." McAllister's look was cynical. "I'm not about to leap from the sun deck, so don't believe any suicide notes you might find beside my still-twitching remains."

"Fat chance of that," Adam told him inelegantly. "You're too stubborn to die. I can see you arguing at the pearly gates over their entrance requirements." He essayed a mock salute. "Happy hunting, friend. If you get in trouble, just ask yourself what agent 007 would do in the circumstances."

McAllister grinned unwillingly at his retreating back.

"Is there something you wanted, Mr. McAllister?" The purser's stocky form materialized at Jim's side.

"Only your good wishes, Leon." Jim moved slowly toward the stairs.

"*Prego?*" the purser asked in confusion. "But of course, you have those. Nothing else?"

"If you're stocking minor miracles, I'll take a couple. Otherwise, forget it."

Leon watched him go down the stairs whistling, and then shook his head sadly. Those tetanus shots obviously had side effects the medical authorities didn't know about. Perhaps he should call on Maria and tell her about it over a cup of coffee. His expression brightened. It was seldom business combined so well with pleasure.

The shore excursion to Byblos started in innocuous fashion.

Jim boarded the bus promptly after lunch, only to be told by the driver that the tour would be delayed because some passengers were still in the dining salon. Nodding resignedly, he strode back toward a seat in the rear of the coach.

Adam and Carla were seated halfway back, holding an earnest conversation with the Altoses, across the aisle. Lisa was just behind them, occupying a window seat with Ceranini beside her. She was deep in a thick book on the Mediterranean and didn't look up as he passed.

Albert Rousch had a seat to himself in the back. He was perspiring freely as he tried to open the window beside him.

"If they say air-conditioning," his voice rose in protest, "then they should turn it on. No air-conditioning, then we should open the windows."

"I'm with you," Jim agreed, taking the seat across the aisle and wishing he'd changed to shorts instead of wearing cotton trousers, which were already sticking to his legs.

"Why are we waiting?" Rousch gave a final, unyielding pull at the window catch and sank down in his seat. "If I do not eat all my lunch so that I am on time, why do I have to wait for someone still eating?" He set about fanning himself with the Tirolean hat.

For a thief, Rousch was a remarkably straight-thinking man, and Jim nodded in full sympathy. Another trickle of perspiration ran down his back and he stirred uncomfortably. Down the aisle, Ceranini was beginning to look restless, too, as Lisa continued to concentrate on her book. Served him right. Imagine taking a sight-seeing trip in your home town just to keep on the right side of a woman! What a pity the blighter didn't do some work instead of hanging around on jaunts like this. It suddenly occurred to him that the sight-seeing bus was under the jurisdiction of Ceranini's firm. In that case, why didn't the man round up the strays and get the thing going?

At that moment, Leon bobbed up the steps of the bus and announced brightly, "We'll leave soon. The guide is coming with the Wittens just now."

An irate-looking Lebanese girl wearing dark glasses was shepherding Frau Witten down the gangway with brisk efficiency. Young Herr Witten was right behind, clutching a banana.

Leon took a seat beside the driver, and the guide slammed the door behind her tardy passengers before picking up the microphone attached to the public address system.

"Bonjour mesdames et messieurs, guten Tag, good afternoon, e buon giorno." She moved rapidly into her welcoming speech in four languages. In the middle of the Italian version, Leon reached over to pull her down to his side. After a whispered consultation, she straightened and continued in English. "Your purser has told me that it will not be necessary to use all four languages and for the rest of the afternoon, I will continue in English and German only." She rattled the same explanation to Frau Witten in German, and Jim decided that both versions sounded like double talk. From Frau Witten's puzzled expression, it seemed that the guide's German accent left as much to be desired as her English pronunciation.

"The area of Lebanon is 3400 square miles," she was saying in a sing-song voice as they went through the port gate, "and our population is half Christian and half Moslem. We will be driving to Byblos by way of our main highway, reaching there in approximately one-half hour. From artifacts unearthed, we believe that Stone Age man built the first city on that site about 6000 years ago. It was a Phoenician city-state some 3000 years ago. Later, the Greeks named it Biblos for their trade in papyrus ... the root for the modern word bible. When the town was captured by crusaders in 1103, it was called Giblet."

By this time, the driver had turned away from the business section of the city and was headed north. James noted that Lisa had finally put down her book to listen, but was staring out the bus window at the traffic on their four-lane freeway. At her side, Ceranini had given up and closed his eyes. McAllister gave a grunt of satisfaction and tuned back in on the guide's spiel.

"Exports of Lebanon include gold, silver, brasswork, furniture, fruit . . ."

"And imports include XIIth Dynasty Egyptian collars," mused Jim, wondering where in the hell Rousch had hidden it.

" . . . mutton is the most popular meat. No pork is served except on Christian tables. French, Arabic, and English are the three languages of our country. The famous cedar tree of Lebanon is pictured on our flag. Perhaps you will remember that in the Old Testament, the cedar stood for holiness, eternity, and peace."

She switched into the German version and

James switched off his listening in the way a television viewer tunes out the commercials. He glanced across at Rousch, who was looking studiously out the window, his eyes half-closed against the sun's glare. Down the aisle, Carla had her trusty camera trained on the passing scenery.

"The modern buildings on your left are the famous Casino du Liban."

All heads, with the exception of Ceranini's, swiveled simultaneously to view the modern opulence of the famous gaming palace.

"There is a magnificent floor show—suitable for adults only." The guide gave Master Witten a quelling look as he started to drop his banana peeling on the floor, then thought better of it. "And gambling of all types. Patrons come from every country in the world. Please make arrangements with your purser if you would like to be part of our night club tour while you are in port."

Give her full marks for the commercial, thought Jim with admiration. Ceranini should pay her a bonus for drumming up business even if she does speak English with a Roumanian accent.

"Our road now follows a rocky promontory. The reeds you see at the roadside hide plantations of mulberry trees. If you have any questions about the country as we drive along, I will try to answer them." The German playback followed, and then the microphone was clicked off and the guide sat down in the seat behind Leon.

Another twenty minutes elapsed before the driver turned into the town of Byblos and parked the bus in the shade of an olive grove.

The guide reached for her microphone again. "Before you leave the bus for independent sight-seeing . . ."

Thank God for small favors, McAllister thought ungraciously.

" . . . may I call your attention to the Egyptian temple of the XIIth Dynasty."

James riveted his attention on Rousch's face, which betrayed no emotion whatsoever at the pronouncement.

". . . crusader buildings include the Frankish castle with the terrace roof for viewing and the Churches of St. John and St. Thecla. The beautiful harbor is below, and restaurants can be found there if you get hungry. Please be back at the bus in two hours."

And be sure to scrape your shoes before coming through the door, Jim finished the sentence silently. Why did all sight-seeing guides have to sound like schoolmarms burdened with retarded children?

"Are you going to look at the castle?" Rousch had heaved himself erect.

McAllister moved over to the aisle, wishing he could stand under a cold shower instead. "You bet," he said trying to infuse his tone with some enthusiasm.

202

"Perhaps we could look together."

"Sure, be glad to. You go ahead." He followed Rousch down the aisle toward the door and glanced around as they went down the bus steps.

Ceranini and Lisa were trudging off arm in arm toward the Church of St. John. McAllister's mouth firmed to a determined line. If she had any sense, she'd certainly stay off the parapets and out of dark corners. Fortunately, the Wittens looked as if they were about to embark on the same path.

Rousch was putting his hat on. "Shall we visit the castle or the churches first?"

Jim fought an urge to follow Lisa and said casually, "You name it."

There was a smirk on the other's face. "Then we'll go to the castle. It would be bad to—how do you say it?—cramp Sandro's style."

The square-cut stones of the ancient crusaders' castle towered over the gravel path in front of them. Over the years, sparse tufts of vegetation had grown in the dirt which the wind had blown against the sides of the fortress, making it seem as if natural forces were waging their own war to reduce the man-made object back to its original state.

"It's amazing that those plants can survive," Jim said, looking at the green sprouts clinging to the native stone in the manner of ivy clinging to old brick.

Rousch nodded as he paused to catch his breath on the steep path to the entrance.

Most of the castle had fallen in ruins, but the elements and archaelogists had been kind in preserving a good part of the façade. The missing parts gave a bombed-out effect, which did not detract from the dignity of the structure as a whole. Instead, the glimpse of sunlight and blue sky as they peered upward through the massive vaulted doorway provided illumination for the magnificent stone arches in the background. Even the brown weeds clinging stubbornly to the edges of the pathway made a color contrast to enchant a painter.

For the better part of an hour, McAllister and Rousch toured the ruin, stopping from time to time in order to admire a pharaoh's foot carved laboriously in stone or parts of a sarcophagus made from the same material. Halfway through the tour of inspection, Leon joined them.

"I'm escaping from the Witten family," he explained. "The boy is determined to commit suicide from a balcony or a stairway." He made an expressive gesture with his hands. "After pulling him back from the edge the last time, I decided that my duties as a purser did not include rescue on land. I hope you don't mind if I join you."

"The more the merrier," McAllister told him, "although we're taking this pretty slowly if you're not keen on antiquities. We were trying to decide the date of this carving." He pointed to a section profiling an ancient pharaoh.

Leon pursed his lips. "It looks like one of the funerary furnishings left over from the royal tombs of Byblos; I should say about eighteenth century B.C. The crusaders evidently gathered some souvenirs while they were here. There are others like it in the National Archaeological Museum in Beirut."

"Are they worth seeing?"

"By all means. They have a remarkable collection of axes made from electrum and some fine Phoenician jewelry and statuettes of gold."

Jim frowned. "What do you mean by electrum?"

Rousch cut in, "It's an alloy, three-quarters gold and one-quarter silver." He pulled off his hat and started fanning himself. "Let's move out on that battlement and get some air."

He pointed toward a long, open balcony with a foot-high parapet providing an uneven border. The erosion caused by winds and weather made it look like an ancient, upended comb with great sections of teeth missing.

They climbed a short flight of sloping stone steps to reach it and moved instinctively over to the low edge so they could look at the ground some thirty feet below.

Jim whistled and stepped back hurriedly to safer footing. "Better watch it; they could use a guard rail on this. If the crusaders persuaded any ladies to come up here late at night and look at the stars, I hope they brought a torch along."

Rousch gave him a disapproving look. "Crusaders had more serious things on their minds than romance."

"They probably had their moments just the same. After all, those quests lasted almost two hundred years, so they must have celebrated on an occasional Saturday night." Jim surveyed the battlement and then moved over to kneel before one of the upright sections. "Take a look at this crusader's cross cut in the stone merlon; evidently this section was used as a sentry tower as well."

The other two got down beside him to examine the meticulous design in the weathered stone.

"Pretty good size," Jim said, thrusting his hand in the aperture.

Rousch nodded. "That was to allow sufficient scope for their arrows."

Jim got to his feet. "I don't see any gutters for the flaming oil they poured down on the enemy."

"You've seen too many Hollywood epics," Leon smirked. "For that sort of thing, you should visit Mont St. Michel along with the other tourists."

A peculiar gleam appeared in McAllister's eyes, but he merely said mildly, "You're probably right. Well, I could do with something long and cool to drink. How about you fellows?"

Rousch emitted a prodigious sigh of relief. "I am in complete agreement; the churches will have to wait for another day." He nodded toward the view in front of them. "We can find a restaurant down by the harbor."

"Or a bar where they stock something besides arak," Leon agreed genially.

Jim fell into step beside him as they started down toward the main entrance. "That's the national drink, isn't it? How is it for taste?"

The purser shrugged. "Not too bad. The appearance puts one off at the beginning. As soon as you add water to it—it looks as if you'd ordered a glass of milk. The fact that it smells like a licorice sweet doesn't help."

Rousch snorted unkindly. "Leon prefers scotch, anything else is a waste of time."

"That's right, I'm probably prejudiced. You should try the arak, Mr. McAllister. A visit to Lebanon isn't complete without it."

"I'll do that."

"And if you have time, sample some of the native dishes. I can recommend the *moghrabie*. It's chicken seasoned with saffron. The *birma* is very good too—a sort of spiral pastry made with nuts. People of the Mideast are fond of sweets."

"They've had a long time to enjoy them," Jim put in casually. "Sugar was one of the discoveries brought from the Moslems by the crusaders. Isn't that right, Rousch?"

"Umm, I suppose so." The man paused in the entrance to wipe the perspiration from his cheeks with an already damp handkerchief. He clamped his hat securely in place before they stepped out in the hot sun and started down a path to the harbor area.

"They have a good-sized fleet of fishing boats in that cove," Jim said.

Leon put on a pair of dark glasses. "I've heard the crews can store part of their catch in the natural caves near the harbor so it's doubly convenient."

"You're quite an expert on this part of the world," Jim said admiringly.

The purser immediately made a deprecatory gesture. "You forget, I spent much of the afternoon listening to our guide advise Frau Witten."

Rousch increased his stride on scenting liquid refreshment nearby, much in the same way a hired saddle horse would move faster on the way back to the barn. He pointed down the path. "There's a fair-looking place." A small building was perched on the edge of the hill overlooking the picturesque boat-filled harbor beneath. Alongside the building, a waist-high stone wall surrounded tables grouped for outdoor eating. Silvered olive trees planted beside the wall provided dappled shade for the patrons, and as the three men drew nearer, they saw that the entire shore excursion party had apparently switched its allegiance from culture to comfort.

James uttered an unconscious sigh of relief as he saw Lisa toying with a soft drink near the entrance, listening in silence to an attentive Sandro. Adam and Carla were watching the proceedings from a round table nearby.

The Wittens and the Altoses were in the middle of sampling *mezzé,* an elaborate Lebanese hors d'oeuvre service while their exhausted guide sagged against the buffet table.

Everyone looked up as the three men approached.

"Come and join us, Jim," Adam called. "Carla's been wondering where you were."

"Thanks. If you gentlemen will excuse me," Jim began courteously.

Rousch waved a careless hand as he headed for an empty table and Leon nodded pleasantly before he followed in the other's wake.

McAllister sank into a rickety wooden chair. "My God, I'm tired. What are you two drinking?"

"Eeeenglish geen," Carla told him. "That's the pronunciation the waiter gives it. His name's Hany and he's that nice-looking man in the tasseled fez who's coming this way."

"Tasseled tarboosh," Adam corrected. "What'll you have, Jim?"

"The same, thanks." McAllister gestured toward their glasses.

"Very good, sir," Hany replied in fair-to-middling English. "Would the gentlemen like something to eat? We have the nice roast of mutton with stuffed squash."

Jim shuddered inwardly at the thought of roast mutton in the afternoon heat. "Not this time, thanks. Perhaps we can come back some evening."

"If the gentleman likes. We fix special for you."

"I'll remember. Just gin and tonic now, thanks."

Hany bowed deeply and withdrew.

"He's making for Rousch's table. I wonder if our prime suspect will be able to depart from this alcoholic oasis under his own power?" Carla mused.

"I hope so." Jim pulled his chair around to settle more comfortably in the shade. "He's too big to carry up that hill. If he gets soused, the guide will have to get the bus driver to come down here and pour him aboard."

"Let's not worry about that until the time comes," Adam said. "How did your afternoon go?"

"The only thing I can state positively is that Rousch didn't retrieve any packages. How about your pals across the way?"

"More of the same," Carla groused. "After we spent an hour going through the castle, Mrs. Altose and I researched the local tourist emporium."

"And?"

"She brought a crèche made of olive wood and a chess set of ivory for her husband. Since they didn't have any wrapping paper, she stuffed both purchases in that bulging tote bag. No jewelry of any kind." She saw him raise his eyebrows. "It's all right; I know about the missing collar and the bracelets too. Never underestimate the sneaky tactics of a good journalist. I've only read pretty meager descriptions of the missing articles, but certainly enough to have known if Mrs. Altose was trying to collect anything suspicious in the tourist shop. It was a total blank."

McAllister looked over at Adam. "How about your quarry?"

The older man shook his head. "All I learned was that Altose knows a great deal about the Mideast. Saying he's a hobbyist in archaeology is like saying Schweitzer was an amateur organist."

Jim nodded and watched as a waiter deftly put his drink in front of him. He lifted the glass and took a satisfying swallow before saying, "This is a fabulous place, isn't it? It makes it difficult to keep your mind on business. I can't see why all tourists don't make tracks for Lebanon."

"Mmmm," Carla uttered in contented agreement. "I haven't seen white sand beaches like that since Australia. And when you combine it with that gorgeous turquoise-colored sea . . ."

"Plus a sprinkling of palm trees and olive groves on the purple hills in the background," contributed Adam.

" . . . you've got the makings of Utopia," Jim concluded. "The harbor would be great for anchoring pleasure craft." Mentally, he was tying up his sloop to a stone-finger pier.

"That harbor was the crusaders' original reason for choosing this site for their fortress," Adam told him. "The small opening to the sea made it possible to repulse enemy invasion fleets. In earlier times, the inhabitants used the protected cove to start their rafts of Lebanese cedars down the coast to treeless Egypt."

"Well, I envy them, no matter what their reason. It's a magnificent stretch of water."

"Have you noticed how peaceful everything is?" Carla asked.

"Peaceful at the moment," Adam agreed, "but in this part of the world, the fuse on some dynamite is usually burning just out of sight."

"Which brings us back to square one, and our friend Mr. Rousch," Jim said. "There isn't much time for the problem to resolve itself before the *Lucarno* sails for Marseilles."

"I'm inclined to think the whole thing's a fizzle," Thorson said in a discouraged tone, "and it's a great pity. The collar and bracelets were a magnificent treasure, and now that they've been stolen they'll undoubtedly disappear into a private collection away from the eyes of the world. It could be hundreds of years before they come to light again."

Carla was looking over at Rousch's table as he spoke. "Well, our suspect isn't suffering from visible qualms of conscience. He's nibbling on hors d'oeuvres and ordering what must be about his third drink."

"Drowning his sorrows . . ."

She made a rude noise. "Not so you'd notice. Even Leon looks disgusted. Poor man, he's having a rude introduction to Mediterranean cruising on passenger freighters."

"Probably wishes he was back with his relatives in the Bronx," Jim said, sitting forward in his chair to allow the breeze to filter onto his back. His gaze wandered around the courtyard. "Any luck with Ceranini?"

Adam shrugged. "I don't know. Lisa hasn't had an opportunity to get away."

"Maybe she doesn't want to."

"Be fair, Jim," Carla said. "If you take a gander, you'll notice that Sandro's making all the overtures. Lisa's just listening."

At the table across the way, Lisa *was* listening, and it seemed that Sandro's insistent voice had drummed in her ears forever.

"We can leave the ship after dinner," he was saying, "and then get a cab out to the casino. There's no point in getting there too early because the first show isn't until ten. Afterwards, we'll try our luck at the tables for a while and then have some supper. How does that sound?"

The cessation of noise made a greater impact on her consciousness than his actual words. Her head jerked up and she scrambled mentally to recall what in the world he'd been talking about.

"If you're not hungry, we can just be driven back to the ship. I'll show you the promontory above Pigeon's Grotto in the moonlight."

His final words registered. "I don't like to take up so much of your time, Sandro," she demurred. "Are you sure you wouldn't rather get back to your apartment? You must have lots of things to catch up on after you've been away so long."

He reached across the table to squeeze her hand fondly. "I would much rather be with you, darling."

She found rubbing her ear gave her an excuse to pull her fingers from under his. It was strange how her pulse rate didn't increase an iota during these tender interludes with Sandro. She had spent the afternoon trying to use evasive tactics without being obvious about it. In every dark corner, his arm had started to slide around her waist, and every steep stair had been an excuse to clutch her hand firmly against his side. At the moment, she felt like consigning him and James McAllister to eternal suffering so she could go back to simple problems like fiscal budgets and irate superiors.

She looked over at Adam's table and encountered James's glance fixed cynically and unwaveringly on her. Her eyes dropped hurriedly and, to her disgust, she felt a blush creep over her cheeks. Damn the man! All he had to do was look at her from across a patio and she all but collapsed on the floor. Dimly, she was aware of Sandro's chattering on again; certainly he was never at a loss for words. All she had to do was nod occasionally to keep the flow coming.

Quite a different case from one James McAllister, whose best friend couldn't claim that he had a gift for social chit-chat. Instead, one was apt to be at drawn daggers with the man in the space of thirty seconds. It was a wonder he had any friends at all—or was she being completely fair about things.

Relentlessly Lisa's memory played back to his painstaking kindness that night in her cabin, the tender care he had shown on the way back from the villa in Iskanderun. It was more than kindness really, rather it was the protective cherishing a man reveals to the one important woman in his life. Instinct told her that; willful prejudice couldn't change it.

Her thoughts raced on, unbidden, to relive that long embrace by his cabin door. She blushed anew at the memory, and Sandro, seeing her red cheeks, preened himself for being such a success with the ladies.

Lisa stared fixedly at the table. If she had any sense, any sense whatever, she'd be remembering the unforgivable insults James had heaped on her. Surely she wasn't such a masochist as to delight in the sort of treatment he handed out. Even if he simmered down to normal behavior, there was no doubt that he would have the final word in any relationship. The possession of a wife wouldn't make the slightest difference. Her heart pounded at the thought and then resumed its normal plodding. Obviously, the last thing that stubborn Florida lawyer wanted at this stage of his existence was a wife. Adam's warning couldn't have been more explicit.

She clenched her palms so tightly in her lap that her knuckles showed white. Of course she had been warned. She was also old enough to know the score with perennial bachelors, even if they were rugged and stubborn devils. So why, and again her nails bit sharply into the soft flesh of her palms, why did she have to be such an unutterable fool as to go and fall head over heels in love with one?

A soft defenseless sigh escaped her lips as the truth was finally acknowledged. At least, there would be no more rationalizing, and with luck, no one would ever know. No one, that is, except herself. How ironic that it took about six hours to fall in love with a man and yet it could very easily take the rest of her life to try and forget him.

"I thought that tomorrow we could go to Baalbek." Sandro's voice surfaced again. "If we get away in mid-morning, we can have lunch on the way and be back in the late afternoon."

"Baalbek?" Lisa said vaguely, as if coming back from another planet.

Ceranini gave her a sharp look. "Baalbek, of course. Probably the finest Roman temple ruin in the world today. Who is the archaeologist . . . you or I?"

"Sorry," her smile was apologetic, "for a moment I wasn't thinking. Does it take long to get there?"

"I just told you, cara. With a comfortably late start and a pleasant lunch, we can still get back in late afternoon. The road up the Bekaa valley is very good and I'll take my own car so we don't have to keep to a schedule. No more of these tourist buses." He looked scornfully at the rest of the group.

"This afternoon's trip has been pleasant." She felt bound to defend her fellow passengers for some reason. "And there's certainly enough room in this cafe so we can all be on our own." As she glanced around, she caught sight of a bedraggled tomcat crouched at the base of the wall next to Rousch's table. It was chewing vigorously on some dust-covered tidbit while keeping a sharp eye on the hors d'oeuvres table in case anything else edible dropped within range.

"Good heavens, that's the mangiest-looking cat I've ever seen," she exclaimed, her shoulders shaking with laughter. "Those tattered ears make him look as if he's been in a fracas every night of his life."

Sandro looked over and nodded absently. "There are others like him down on the dock. The fishermen feed them when they bring in their catches."

"I'll bet he's a dandy fighter—probably the scourge of the neighborhood."

"Undoubtedly he has an interesting ancestry," Ceranini said in bored tones. "Do you agree to my plans for Baalbek then?"

She brought her glance back to his intent face. If she didn't go to Baalbek with him, it would mean another excursion under James's scathing glances.

"All right, Sandro." She tried to instill the proper enthusiasm in her voice. "The day should be very nice. I hope the weather stays fine."

He leaned back, satisfied. "You don't have to worry about that here. Our climate is one of the reasons the Syrians come to Lebanon for their holidays."

"Ladeez, gentlemen—pliss!" The raised voice of their guide interrupted all conversation in the courtyard. "It is time for us to go. The driver has parked our bus in front of the restaurant. Would you take your places, pliss, in the next ten minutes."

While Sandro went in search of Hany to pay their bill, Lisa wandered out to the roadside to stand by the bus. Carla hurried through the doorway to catch up with her.

"Did you survive the Lebanese smorgasbord?" she wanted to know.

Lisa smiled. "I wasn't hungry, just thirsty. Lemonade's the same the world over."

Carla moved closer to say in low tones, "How's it going with the Latin lover?"

"He's having difficulties. Every time he found a dark corner in the church, I was pointing out evidences of Byzantine culture or an earlier synagogue."

The older woman laughed. "Like trying to make love to an encyclopedia. If it weren't for your hair and figure, he'd have deserted you for our guide early in the tour."

Lisa saw James and Adam approaching, with Sandro close behind them. She summoned a brilliant smile and moved over to the door of the bus to intercept Ceranini. "I was just telling Carla about your plans for visiting the casino tonight." Catching a glimpse of James's dour expression, she went on enthusiastically, "You'll have to explain about the gaming tables, Sandro; I haven't even been to Las Vegas for practice."

His look was expansive and he reached over to put a proprietary arm around her shoulders. "Never mind, we'll play for fun then. With someone as lovely as you around, I would find it impossible to concentrate on the games of chance."

Digest that one, Mr. McAllister, Lisa thought triumphantly, taking her seat in the bus. She looked away as James walked, or rather stomped, down the aisle past her. Then, leaning back, she bit her lips to keep them from trembling. She'd show him that she didn't need his help—now or ever!

After the strenuous afternoon, the trip back to Beirut could only come as an anticlimax. Conversation lapsed; even the Altoses were sitting back with closed eyes, their faces expressing a common wish to be in their air-conditioned stateroom rather than a bumpy tourist bus. Leon shared a front seat with the guide, who gave the impression that the half day spent with Frau Witten's son had taken a good ten years off her life. In their seats across from her, the Germans seemed tired but happy. Mama was resting with a handkerchief over her eyes while B.B. clutched an unopened bottle of lemonade. Evidently, Lisa reasoned, this was in case the bus had engine trouble on the way home and delayed dinner. There was a boy who planned ahead!

It was just before the dinner hour when the bus finally pulled up on the pier alongside the *Lucarno*.

Sandro kept Lisa's elbow in a firm grasp while they thanked their guide and driver before strolling across to the ship's gangway. A stocky individual in the brown uniform of the

Lebanese customs service waited by the bottom of the steps.

"Mr. Ceranini?"

"Yes?" Sandro's only reaction was a slight frown.

"I have been waiting to see you. There are some irregularities in connection with your cargo on board."

The frown deepened. "Irregularities? I don't understand. The same procedure has been followed when I have shipped similar cargo from Italy before."

The guard's shrug was a monument of indifference. "That may be. However, if you want this unloaded tomorrow as planned, you must check with my superiors tonight. I suggest you bring all invoices and records. About eight o'clock at our office on the pier." He started to walk away.

"Just a minute! You can't order me to . . ."

"About eight." The guard didn't even bother to turn and look at Ceranini as he spoke.

"Dio!" Sandro slammed a clenched fist into his palm with a resounding smack. "What do those imbeciles want now?"

"I'm sorry—," Lisa began.

He looked down into her upturned face as if just aware of her presence. "So am I." His voice was disgusted. "I must have words with Leon, but it looks as if our plans for the evening are ruined. These customs difficulties can take all night."

221

"It doesn't matter. I'll live without seeing the inside of the casino."

He squeezed her hand gratefully. "I'll try to make it up to you tomorrow, Lisa. Now, if you'll excuse me, I must check with the purser's department and see how they've listed my cargo on their bills of lading. Some idiot must have made a mistake on the valuation." He lifted her fingers to his lips for a gentle caress and then turned to hurry up the gangway.

She watched him go and then moved to go aboard herself. She collided with a solid body and felt familiar hands clamp onto her waist until she regained her footing.

"You!" Startled, she stared back at James's impassive countenance. "It would be."

"I didn't mean to knock you down." He motioned her up the gangway. "After all, you've had one bitter blow already this evening."

There was a pause and Lisa could feel his amused gaze boring into her back as she went up the incline ahead of him.

"It was too bad Ceranini ran into all this trouble, but you can never tell when these customs fellows will get their backs up." His voice was bland, too bland. "Yes ma'am, I'm certainly sorry about that."

"I'll bet you are," she gritted out. Once in the corridor, she glanced around to see that it was deserted before she stopped and confronted him. "Look, if this is your sadistic sense of humor coming to the fore, you don't have to go to such extremes."

"Don't I?" The blandness had disappeared with one of his abrupt changes of manner. "This isn't a tea party, you know. There's a devil of a lot of money involved in this theft and I think we're about at the point where something's going to move. When this is all over, I'd like to see you get back to the States in good condition. Until then, your social life will have to suffer."

"So it was your doing. . . ."

He raised his eyebrows. "Not really. Ceranini did it himself; I merely called the customs men's attention to a few requirements he had neglected to satisfy." Reaching down, he plucked her stateroom key from her fingers and walked down the hall until he reached her door. "Nothing serious, but it should take him the better part of the night to get everything in order."

"While I sit and twiddle my thumbs."

"That's up to you. It's better than having your neck stretched in a dark alley while you're out doing the town." He turned her key in the lock and opened the door for her. "You can always read a good book and improve your mind."

She snatched the key he was dangling. "Any other suggestions?"

"Not now. I'll make up my mind by tomorrow whether your Baalbek excursion seems advisable." He ignored her indrawn breath of temper. "Don't try any monkey business. I've got enough on my mind without playing games with you."

"When I want you to play games . . ." she began in a trembling voice.

" . . . you'll let me know. In the meantime, you'll also do as you're told." The expression on his face softened as he went on to say quietly, "Please Lisa, I need your help with this." Then he turned and disappeared down the corridor.

Lisa walked slowly into her stateroom. She dropped her purse on the bedspread and ran a thoughtful hand through her hair. When Lieutenant McAllister dropped his arrogant pose, he could become very human indeed. That "please" had been a master stroke of diplomacy.

Her eyes focused on a familiar glass figure standing in his accustomed place on top of her dressing table. Shadrach was back in occupancy!

Evidently James had persuaded the friendly bedroom steward that the camel belonged in her cabin rather than his. She stood transfixed in the middle of the room, uncertain whether to laugh or cry. Why did he bother with such gestures? Was it another apology, another effort toward peaceful coexistence? Adam had probably convinced him to gloss over their quarrel rather than prolonging it, and

Shadrach was the first offering toward restoring the status quo.

She moved over to run a gentle finger down the camel's haughty nose, and in doing so noted the folded piece of paper shoved under his base. Her fingers were shaking by the time she'd smoothed it out. A firm masculine hand had copied an old Arab proverb, "There are three things that can never be hidden: a mountain, one riding a camel, and the face of a man in love."

Nothing else. Not even a signature. Yet, at that moment, Lisa wouldn't have exchanged it for the jewel-encrusted volume of the *Gospels of Charlemagne*.

CHAPTER TEN

"I do not understand you, Lisa," Sandro complained the next day as they drove back toward Beirut on the mountain highway from the northeast.

"What's the difficulty? I didn't mean to disturb you." Lisa fastened her head scarf more securely and scrunched down in the seat of Sandro's open sports car.

"Then how can you spend the day with me and yet not be with me?"

"You make me sound like Houdini or a ghost haunting some ancestral hall." She smiled at him. "I'm very much with you."

"You don't think I'm serious." He glanced over at her and then asked with concern, "Is there too much wind for you? Would you like me to put the top up?"

"No, I'm fine, thanks."

"You're sure?" He noted her admirable profile and then her lack of response. "I could stand on my head," he went on smoothly. "It's one of our tourist attractions—really remarkable. How would you like that?"

"Whatever you say, Sandro," she murmured,

glancing at her watch. "Do you think we'll be back at the ship in time for dinner?"

"I give up." With a squeal of tires, he pulled the car over to the side of the road and stared at her. "You're still not paying any attention. Earlier, I thought you were not interested in Baalbek." He shook his head regretfully. "Now I realize you are not happy in my company."

"I'm sorry if I've been rude, Sandro. I didn't mean to be. Don't you think we'd better drive on?"

"In a minute. We're not really wasting time," he told her sardonically, "you can look at that cedar tree in the fenced area to your right."

Obediently she stared over to where he indicated. "Is it a cedar of Lebanon?"

"One of them. There are only about 400 left in the entire country. The government feels very protective about them." He shot her a brooding look. "What's the matter, Lisa? What makes you different today?"

"Stop being absurd. I thoroughly enjoyed seeing Baalbek."

"So much that you wanted to skip the Temple of Bacchus entirely and come back to the ship early."

"I don't know why you're making such a fuss. It was hot up there in the ruins."

"Even later, when I took you to the finest place to eat in the Bekaa valley and we had a shaded table on the patio . . . when I ordered

227

the most splendid roast mutton, washed down with arak . . . you had no interest."

"I wasn't hungry," she said feebly.

"That's what I mean!" He slapped his forehead dramatically. "You don't even remember; we ate cold chicken accompanied by a very good Italian wine. No, I must face the truth. How do you say it, Lisa? I've lost my touch."

"Oh Sandro, stop it." She felt like laughing at his crestfallen expression but didn't want to hurt him further. For a compromise, she reached out and touched his hand impulsively. "I hope you'll forgive me, I've had other things on my mind today."

He put his hand over hers. "Things like another man."

She drew back. "We should get on."

"Very well, cara, but you aren't fooling me." He looked in the side mirror for a break in the traffic and then pulled out with an acceleration that snapped her head back. They drove for some distance in silence before he said defiantly, "I had hoped this might be a beginning . . . not an ending. I do not like to lose."

Lisa had the feeling that his pride was damaged far more than his heart, but she was careful not to let any amusement show in her voice. "Be fair, Sandro. You can't lose what you've never had. It was only for fun right from the beginning."

"Perhaps in the beginning." He twisted her words deliberately as he passed a car slowing for a turn. "But then I changed my mind." His sharp glance raked her profile again. "Evidently you did too." A spurt of amusement crept into his tone. "American women can't be trusted."

"They're about the same in their thinking as Italian men," she assured him. "Are you having dinner aboard?"

"Dio no! I do not intend to go within shouting distance of that customs office again."

As they turned into the port area a half hour later he said, "You can tell Mr. McAllister that I am planning to be a model citizen from now on, so he can bother someone else with the minor government officials. I cannot afford any more import taxes."

"I'll give him the message, but are you sure he'll know what I'm talking about?"

"Very sure." He let the car drift to a stop by the *Lucarno*'s gangway. Then he deliberately pulled her close to him for a thoroughly efficient if passionless kiss. "There!" he said with satisfaction as he let her go. "You can also tell Mr. McAllister he owed me that."

"I won't have to." She smiled at him and got out of the car accompanied by a chorus of whistles from the ship. "All the crew lining the rail will be happy to spread the news. Arrivederci, Sandro. If you're ever in Los Angeles again—"

"I'll call and see if you have a friend. Arrivederci, carissima." He gave a mocking salute and drove away.

So much for Sandro, she thought strolling toward the ship. One down and one to go. The one to go was apt to be far more difficult, especially if he had been looking on a moment before.

Good-natured smiles from the Italian crew greeted her as she reached the deck. Love made the world go round as they saw it, and a lingering kiss on the dock was the same as a chaste salute on the boat deck at midnight. An American man's reaction wouldn't have been as tolerant, she decided as she made her way down to her cabin, so it was just as well that James hadn't been in the audience.

She stopped in the middle of unlocking her door. There was no valid reason to believe that he was even aboard ship. He had made a hurried remark at breakfast that the Baalbek visit was all right but to keep her eyes open, and then had dashed off without finishing his coffee.

Lisa opened the door to her stateroom and went in. Evidently the steward had done a special cleaning job, because a newly ironed spread was atop her bed and the articles on her dressing table were pushed into tidy piles. Shadrach stared back at her from his place in front of the mirror. Lisa grinned, feeling unaccountably cheered by the sight of his bulky figure.

She started in surprise at the sound of a determined knocking on the hall door. "Come in," she called.

"Well, I'm glad you're back," Carla said from the doorway. "I was about to perish from loneliness."

"There's no need to. Come on in. What's the matter? Where is everybody?"

"If by everybody, you mean Jim, he's conspicuously absent." She watched Lisa's guilty reaction with amusement. "Adam is also gone. The Altoses went off in a car," she was ticking the list off on her fingers, "ditto dear Mr. Rousch. You had the handsome Sandro. By elimination, that left me with Frau Witten and her charming son. Would you believe I've been listening and saying *ja* to her and that odious child for the better part of the day. My knowledge of German—until this afternoon—consisted of *guten Tag, ja, nein,* and a whistling acquaintance with the 'Beer Barrel Polka.' " She collapsed on the bed. "I'm an absolute wreck— wait till I catch up with Adam! I'll flay him for deserting me."

Lisa's laughter bubbled up. "I'd love to have seen you. Why didn't you just lead them to the dining room?"

"I did keep stuffing the little—did I say little?—wretch with bananas." She pushed her hair back distractedly.

"Didn't the men give any hint of where they were going?"

"Not to me. I believe Adam thought he'd

231

keep me out of trouble that way. He knows that I came on this cruise in hopes of a good story. My managing editor recently got an anonymous tip that the stolen museum pieces were going to be disposed of and it was the kind of story our magazine does best—all headlines and few facts." Her look was frank. "I can't say I'm proud of the type of stuff I've written, but it was a living. That's why Adam brought a gust of fresh air in my life. I intend to make sure he doesn't suffer for it."

Lisa smiled gently. "Now you're being silly. I know Adam has been sending up prayers of thanksgiving ever since he met you. Furthermore, if you don't invite me to the wedding, I'll never forgive you."

"You're a terrible liar, Lisa Halliday, but a darling all the same." Carla steadied her voice with an effort. "What I really came in for," she was trying to sound natural, "was to see if you'd go back to Byblos with me. Since it doesn't look as if I'm going to get the type of story my boss sent me for, I thought I could do an interview with that nice Hany in the restaurant there. You know what I want—'How Lebanese Chefs Use Curdled Milk in Their Fabulous Stews' or 'Let Goat's Milk Do Wonders for Your Waistline.' That sort of malarky. We might as well accomplish something if we're to be deserted for the day."

"Well, I suppose I could," Lisa said hesitantly. "It's strange I didn't see any familiar faces at Baalbek, either."

"How was your trip by the way?"

"I was a complete dud and Sandro resented it."

Carla arched shapely eyebrows. "He resented another man beating him at his own game. I don't think it happens very often to Signor Ceranini. Don't worry, it's probably good for his character."

"It didn't help his disposition." Lisa ran a comb through her hair and gave Carla a thoughtful look in the mirror at the same time. "Are you sure Adam and James won't be angry if we go poking around on our own?"

"I'm not sure," the other said truthfully, "but there's no reason we can't take care of ourselves. We can hire a taxi on the pier and be out there in no time. The interview shouldn't take long, and we can get back here shortly after dark. We'll miss dinner aboard but we could eat at Hany's if we feel like it."

"It sounds all right." Lisa drew a reflective finger along Shadrach's back. Then, straightening, she said, "Let's go. It's awful just waiting for news; I feel I'll go up the wall if I have to mark time in this stateroom."

"Believe me, sitting in the lounge with Frau Witten certainly isn't any better. Grab a sweater for after dark and I'll stop at my cabin to get a note pad. I hope Hany's recipe cards aren't in Arabic."

"I hope so too, unless your Arabic is better than mine."

"Mine is nonexistent, so we're even. Unless Hany's conversions are accurate, I'll be giving Mideast heartburn to thousands of readers." She paused by the door. "Cross your fingers that my editor's wife doesn't try one."

The trip up the coast was uneventful despite the evening traffic on the main north-south road. Congestion caused by a stalled truck made their arrival in Byblos later than they had planned, and Lisa was glancing worriedly at her watch as the taxi pulled up in front of the restaurant.

"We'd better plan on eating here," she told Carla. "Let's tell the driver to wait."

"You tell him, your French is better than mine. Let him know we're hiring him for the evening. Don't worry about the cost—that's what my expense account is for."

"If you say so," Lisa agreed dubiously. "From the look he's giving me, the price is going up right now. Are you sure he can't understand English?"

Carla shrugged. "That's what he claimed. I'll go on in and try to find Hany. At least, I can negotiate with him in English."

"Even so, you'll probably be some time." Lisa glanced at her watch again. "I'd like to see those excavations the French did below the castle and I didn't have time on the tour. Why don't I meet you here in about an hour?"

"Won't it be too dark for sight-seeing?"

"This dusk should last long enough for all I want to do. You go on in and start talking food." She watched Carla turn obediently away and then called softly to her, "When you get around to discussing our dinner with Hany, try to settle on chicken. I've had enough mutton to last me for years."

Carla smiled and nodded before going on.

Lisa's bargaining with the cab driver was pleasantly short; probably because he was looking forward to lazing in his cab and being paid for watching a sunset.

Soon she was making her way up the path toward the deserted promontory under the castle walls, where excavations had shown evidences of several past civilizations. Wandering happily in the rocky field, shadowed by an occasional cypress or olive tree, she examined fallen columns and stones in restful quiet, undisturbed except for the lapping of the surf on the beach far below. Down by the harbor area, she could see minute figures of fishermen working busily by their boats. From her vantage point, it was as if they represented the world of the present, while the quiet field in which she stood held only fabled figures of the past. Over both civilizations, the pink and gold rays of a magnificent sunset were fading delicately into the purple of night.

She looked up to see the tower of the castle silhouetted behind her. It would be wonderful to watch the sunset from a battlement overhead. Her glance traced stone steps leading precariously up the wall; then she passed through a shadowy archway into a rear entrance of the fortress.

She was halfway up before she thought of possible reasons against the move. Even then, her hesitation was brief and she continued carefully up the uneven steps, balancing with her hand against the wall itself when necessary. Ducking into the gloomy arch wasn't pleasant, although the location of the inner stair guaranteed scraped knees rather than a tumble onto the ground itself. Only the merest sliver of light remained on the rough steps to guide her upward. Only that light, and the faint gleam of twilight through the arch at the top, made her fail to reconsider her impulsive move and turn back.

Doggedly she climbed, thankful for her low-heeled pumps. Heels any higher would have been a distinct hazard. What a pity the crusaders couldn't have spent a little more time on their construction, she was thinking. A surprise attack by the enemy in the middle of the night must have resulted in a lot of bruises when they scrambled up those treacherous steps in their suits of armor.

Finally she reached the top of the stairs and moved hesitantly through the arch leading out onto the battlement. The glory of the sunset made her forget everything but the wonder of the moment. Groves of trees and the square stone houses of Byblos were like black paper cutouts on the horizon. The stubby ships with their nets draped alongside looked Biblical, unchanging, as if they had been anchored and bobbing in the gentle waves since before time began.

Carefully, as if afraid to disturb the tranquility of the scene before her, Lisa moved to the edge of the parapet fronting the stone battlement. Her attention stayed focused on the changing colors, the spectacular that nature staged with such easy abandon.

It was some time before an insignificant grating sound penetrated her consciousness. Then, as she moved to turn, a rough hand clamped over her mouth and she was dragged away from the wall into the shadows at the back of the balcony.

Her fists shot out to beat on her captor as she struggled in his grasp. If only she could get free to—

"Lisa, don't! Cut it out or I'll have to clip you!" A low, intense voice was whispering urgently in her ear.

A low, intense, *familiar* voice! Her body sagged in relief and suddenly the man was hanging on to keep her from collapsing at his feet.

"You little nut," a hand was removed and found its way around to cradle the back of her neck. "What the hell are you doing here?" James McAllister asked.

"Being scared out of my wits by you." She was clinging to his coat lapels as if her life depended on it. "Did you have to sneak up behind me?"

"I felt more like tossing you over the parapet," he muttered furiously. "Why in the dickens aren't you aboard ship?"

"Because I came to Byblos with Carla." She gazed at him as if hypnotized, trying to ignore those disturbing fingers at her hairline. "She's down exchanging recipes with Hany at the restaurant."

"I hope to God she stays there. Adam will have a stroke if anybody else stumbles up here."

She pulled away although she missed the support of his strong arms. "I don't understand; why shouldn't I be here?"

"Because we're expecting Rousch at any minute." He pulled her back further into the shadows. "I'd send you down if I didn't think you'd run into him on the way. As it is, you'll stay here out of sight and out of harm's way."

"All right, if you say so." Her whisper was tremulous as she looked around them. "Are we alone up here?"

"Not on your life. We've got security men stashed away in odd corners, but they couldn't take a chance of showing themselves when you decided to join the party."

"How was I to know?" she asked in an aggrieved tone. "You could have left a note aboard ship."

"Sure, or had it broadcast over the public address system every fifteen minutes." His hand shot out to clasp her wrist. "Quiet! I hear someone coming."

They stood close together, motionless as the wall behind them while the sound of deliberate footsteps advanced up the steps, grating on the stone and sand like a soft-shoe dance routine. Perhaps ten seconds passed before a shadowy male figure emerged in the arch, still hunched over from the climb up the uneven stairs.

The man straightened, gave a desultory glance behind him and then moved purposefully toward the center merlon. Kneeling in front of it, he thrust one hand into some sort of opening.

Lisa moved her head to get a better view and decided he was scrabbling in the crusader's cross cut out in the stone. Years before, archers had stood behind it during attacks, but this time it had been used as a cache. There was a muffled exclamation of satisfaction and then the intruder brought out a carefully wrapped bundle. Standing erect, he reached for the flashlight in his rear pocket, switched it on, and directed the beam onto a chamois bag in his hand.

There was another murmur of pleasure as he transferred the bag carefully to the top of the merlon. He shoved the torch carelessly back in his pocket, then used both hands to undo the fastenings on the bag. When it was finally opened, the light came into play again and Lisa caught a glimpse of its reflection on a shimmer of gold and jewels.

She caught her breath in a soundless gasp, not needing James's tightened grasp on her wrist to insure her silence. So the treasure had come to light at last!

But how did they propose to bring this charade to a conclusion? Was Rousch—and it must be Rousch if that silly alpine hat silhouette was any indication—just to calmly walk away? It seemed so. He was carefully securing the fastenings on his bag and tucking it under his arm as he prepared to leave.

As if recognizing potential danger, James pulled Lisa back and tried to push her completely behind him.

The flashlight flickered on and off as if Rousch could not make up his mind whether to risk the beam. Then his memory of the steep staircase must have decided him and the strong light was left on, but pointed cautiously toward his feet.

What happened next was sheer bad luck. Rousch stumbled momentarily over one of the small stones littering the balcony floor and, in regaining his balance, moved the beam of the flash erratically upward to spotlight the hem of Lisa's skirt.

It was hard to believe a portly man could move so fast. In a split second, Rousch was training an ugly, snub-nosed automatic on James and Lisa, the flashlight beam fixed blindingly into their eyes. She heard James growl and felt the hard muscle of his arm tense as he moved a step forward.

"Don't try it," Rousch ordered gutturally, "and don't think you're going to stop me now, McAllister." His accent had thickened perceptibly. "It was thoughtful of you to bring my dear Lisa along."

She felt the strength of James's fingers again as Rousch's meaning became clear.

"Leave Miss Halliday out of this, Rousch. I'll give you my word we won't interfere."

Rousch swore briefly, contemptuously, in reply. "You won't interfere, that I can believe. But how many men have you stationed in the castle?" He let out a wheeze of laughter as silence answered him. "That's what I thought. No, I think I will do much better if I have your friend along. You needn't worry; if she behaves herself, I may release her down on the pier. Naturally, if there is any interference on the way," the light remained trained on McAllister's grim face, "then Miss Halliday unfortunately will become expendable. You understand?" His deliberately slow speech became brisk. "Now, my dear Lisa, come over to me."

"Don't move, Lisa," James commanded flatly.

The end of the automatic moved downward slightly. "Either Miss Halliday comes to me now, Lieutenant, or she comes to me in thirty seconds. After you have been shot in the stomach."

"No! Don't!" Lisa wrenched her wrist from James's hold by brute force. She stumbled across the uneven floor toward the parapet.

"I thought so." Rousch oozed satisfaction. "How very touching." He moved over by her in the shadow of the merlon, carefully keeping the gun trained on McAllister, who stood tensed a body length away. "You'll walk in front of me," he was saying when his foot collided with something in the darkness; a something that emitted a bloodcurdling screech of pain, sending Rousch reeling backward in surprise. At the same moment, James lunged forward and knocked the other's gun hand aside before putting all his weight into a right uppercut to the jaw. There was the sickening crack of bone against bone, and Rousch plummeted downward to measure his length on the dusty floor.

"Oh God, you've killed him," Lisa whimpered.

McAllister took charge of the gun before looking more closely at the still figure on the floor. "He's okay. His head is so hard that it would take more than one punch to crack it. I was just lucky that he was off-balance when I hit him. If you have any sympathy, save it for that poor cat he stepped on."

"I know," she looked around in dazed comprehension. "He's disappeared—I'm not surprised. His poor tail will never be the same again."

"Sure it will. Wharf cats are tough." James was massaging the back of his knuckles absently as he spoke. "They probably scrounge for rodents up in these ruins. I was hoping that you'd seen him."

She nodded wearily. "For once, our ESPs were working on the same channel. The cat seemed our only chance to catch Rousch off guard." Her eyes suddenly glistened with tears as she stared up at him. "You're such a fool—I thought you were going to get yourself shot."

"Well, I didn't," he grinned at her, "so hang onto that chamois bag, will you? We've gone to enough trouble to recover the stuff." He put up his fingers to utter a piercing whistle. "That should bring the rest of them running." As he casually reached over to pick up the flashlight, he asked, "Want to take a look at the loot?"

She heard the sound of footsteps hurrying up the steps and looked down again at Rousch's sprawled figure before she slowly shook her head. "Take it away. I don't care if I never see it. Not even if it were the entire lost treasure of the Incas."

"Don't take it too much to heart, little one."

James's voice was gentle and understanding. "We're about to close up shop."

He was right. It was scarcely a half hour before he and Lisa had the balcony to themselves.

In the meantime, Adam had arrived to take charge of the jewels and deliver them to the British authorities. "After I get them to Her Majesty's representative," he had told Lisa, "I'll go and collect Carla. Maybe an evening on the town will make up for standing her up all day and the loss of her story."

"You mean there's to be no publicity?"

"Definitely no publicity. That was part of the guarantee we made with the Lebanese government. The museum pieces go back to Britain and Rousch goes into a local hospital until his cracks are healed. Then he'll be given a one-way ticket to face criminal charges on the continent."

They watched the inert form loaded on a stretcher before being carried down to the waiting ambulance.

"It was a tremendous gamble for no reward," Lisa said.

Adam nodded. "It generally is. Stealing national treasures makes no sense at all; they're too well known for selling on the open market, so the thief is restricted to dealing with unscrupulous private collectors. Rousch probably did it for revenge as much as anything else. The museum authorities had ticked him off pretty severely for his erratic private life." He shrugged and changed the subject. "We've given the people in Byblos more excitement than they've had since the last invasion."

"I, for one, could do with less excitement and more explanations." Her mood was querulous now that the symptoms of shock were disappearing.

"Ask Jim. He's the one who tumbled to what was happening."

She glanced over to where James was talking to some uniformed policemen. "Mr. McAllister is busy," she said crossly. "He's always busy."

Adam gave her his lopsided smile. "Don't you believe it. Five'll get you ten, he'll find time for everything."

"You're on."

He glanced down at his watch. "I'd better collect Carla before she runs off with that restaurant man. What do you think about my taking her to the casino? We could gamble and get all the vices out of our system before I introduce her to the rigors of academic life."

"It sounds fine. If you win enough at roulette, you can buy your own university."

"Don't say things like that around my intended—she might take you seriously." He ruffled her hair gently. "Thanks Lisa, for your part in this—and for everything."

"Go on with you, Professor." Her voice was uneven as she added gaily, "Just make sure you turn in that loot before you go to the casino and lose all your money."

"You're fresh, too!" He smiled again and went through the archway, the chamois bag firmly in hand.

"Are you ready to go?" James was hovering impatiently at her elbow.

"Yes, of course. What about you?"

"I told them I'd sign a statement for the local authorities tomorrow. As far as our embassy is concerned, I'll have to make a personal report, that's all. Come on—but be careful!" He grabbed her wrist with one hand and appropriated Rousch's flashlight with the other. "There's no point in breaking our necks on these stairs at this point in the production."

She stayed obediently by his side as they wound downward. "I still can't believe it's over. You're sure that Rousch is going to be all right?"

"Absolutely. He may have a small concussion after colliding with the floor, but they'll have him out of Beirut within a week."

"I wonder if he would have pulled the trigger?"

"He probably won't ever admit it now." James's tone was thoughtful as he weighed the possibilities. "I suppose he felt like it—he was so close to success with his plan. Thanks to the cat, we don't have to worry about it any more."

"You're certainly being casual about it, considering you could have been killed!"

"Lisa, Lisa, Lisa." He cupped her ears with his palms and shook her head gently with each word. "You're fussing again. If you don't stop, I'll have to take drastic measures."

"How drastic?" she asked in confusion.

He chuckled. Dropping his hands, he pulled her close to his side momentarily before threatening, "Drastic enough. But let's get off these damned stairs first."

They started down the steps again slowly.

"You didn't have to worry about Rousch getting away," he said. "We had enough men posted around the castle to take care of any escape."

"You were certainly playing a lone hand," she told him heatedly, a little chagrined now that she had made such a proclamation of her concern and affection. "You were darned careful to keep me completely in the dark."

"And much good it did me. Look what I'm letting myself in for."

There was more silence while she digested that remark. As they reached the main entrance of the castle, James switched off the flashlight.

"There should be enough moonlight now to see us down the hill. Would you like to stop for a drink at the restaurant?"

"Hany's? I'd love to. Heavens, I just remembered—Carla and I have a cab waiting there—unless Adam found him."

"It doesn't matter. We'll pick up another

247

one when it's time to get back to Beirut. Beautiful night, isn't it?"

She rounded on him furiously. "James McAllister, you're not going to start in with a discussion of the weather at this point!"

"I didn't think I'd get away with it."

"You certainly won't." The crispness of her tone changed to entreaty. "Will you please tell me what happened?"

"I like that 'please.' You know, for a career woman you show remarkable possibilities." He ducked as she raised a threatening hand. "All right, what do you want to know?"

"Everything, of course. First, how did you know the treasure was up in the castle?"

"That takes a little explaining." He fished for a cigarette, offered Lisa one, and lit them both before going on. "Perhaps it would be easier if I went back to take things in sequence. Incidentally, a good part of this is educated guesswork until Rousch regains consciousness. It all started, of course, when he stole the collar and the bracelets from the museum exhibit. The actual theft wasn't too difficult because of his work with that particular display, but getting rid of the evidence was considerably harder. Obviously he had to have an associate to hide the pieces for him until the furor died down and it was safe to retrieve them. He made arrangements with a partner and went back to England to wait it out, all the while loudly proclaiming his innocence. This summer, he decided to make his move. Somewhere along the line, he must have talked too much. Probably at some party when he was too drunk to be cautious. At any rate, at least three people knew about his decision to retrieve his merchandise."

Lisa counted them off on her fingers. "Altose, I suppose."

"Altose, certainly." Jim drew deeply on his cigarette. "Although Mrs. Altose seems to have been just along for the boat ride."

"Then they are honeymooners?"

"So far as I know." He grinned down at her. "Judging from her type, I think she's too shrewd to settle for anything less than strict legality."

She gave a delicate shudder. "And judging from his type, I'd say she was a fool if she did." She held up another finger. "Carla knew about it too."

"Yes, but hers was strictly a professional interest and came from the front office. Her editor thought it sounded like a good headline piece and sent her off. Little did he know that she was going to take one look at Adam . . ."

"And find her own treasure."

He laughed. "There's sentiment for you! Anyhow, Carla was crossed off the list early in the game. That left only your friend Sandro." The humor was gone from his voice. "He was our favorite suspect until yesterday."

"I knew you didn't trust him," she said hesitantly.

"Trust him, hell! I'd like to have knocked his block off."

They walked a few steps in silence.

"I didn't realize you felt so strongly about him," she managed finally.

"I was surprised myself." The undercurrent of humor was back again. "All I could do was make life uncomfortable for him with the customs people."

"Then he wasn't concerned with the theft?"

James shook his head. "No, Ceranini is one of those characters who enjoy a little graft on the side. Strictly minor league stuff, like trying to cut corners on his import duty. He was trying to see if he could cut into Rousch's game— that's why he was sticking so close to him. It wasn't until the Lebanese officials and the Italian consulate warned him off that he decided the ante was too steep."

"Was that what Altose was trying to do?"

"In the sense that he wanted a piece of the action, yes. When I asked for more details on Mr. Altose, they came up with the information that he was a well-known collector of antiquities. Whether he was trying to deal with Rousch for his personal collection or whether he was representing other interests, we'll have to wait to hear. It was Altose who set the fire in Rousch's stateroom. He claims it was an accident, but it probably was a deliberate warning

250

to Rousch. After we arrived in Beirut, our consulate people brought pressure to bear on Altose. With his past record for semi-shady transactions, he was persuaded to get out while he was still ahead. Or maybe this second marriage has mellowed him. Anyhow, that took care of him."

She stopped in the middle of the path. "All right, I give up. You've thoroughly confused me. Next, you'll be saying it was Frau Witten or Leon."

"Yes."

"Frau Witten?" Lisa was aghast.

"No, idiot—Leon. Come on, let's keep moving. I can smell food."

"Hany's roasting mutton. I might have known," she said with resignation. "Stop walking so fast."

He caught her elbow in a firm grip and forced her to match her steps to his. "In another fifty feet, you can collapse in front of a magnum of champagne for the rest of the night."

"Really!" She smiled but pulled him to a stop again nonetheless. "Finish the explanations first."

"Remember those drastic measures," he threatened and then relented with a grin. "You could have figured it out yourself if you'd used your head and stopped skirmishing with me every hour or so." There was no hiding the amusement in his voice, although a thin cloud over the moon shadowed his face.

"Now listen carefully. It had to be Leon because he was the one with the opportunity all along the line. Although this is his first trip on the *Lucarno*, it didn't take much research to discover that he's been aboard freighters in the Mediterranean for the past five years. He made a mistake when he lectured on Mideast antiquities on the tour; he made another mistake when he stayed so close to Rousch—far too close for an ordinary steamship employee. He wasn't taking any chances on a double cross. Neither was Rousch. Leon had hidden the treasure here in one of the caves in the harbor area. The tides make them fairly tricky to enter, so he didn't have to worry about his hiding place being discovered. To make doubly sure, he could come and check on it each voyage when his ship called in at Beirut. By the time Rousch had found a high bidder for his property, they were ready to move."

"Do you know who that bidder was?"

James shook his head. "Leon wasn't talking when we picked him up earlier this evening. We'd watched him retrieve the loot and followed him up to the castle."

"Was he going to join Rousch?"

"Nope. He was going back to the *Lucarno* and complete the cruise. He'd have a perfect alibi when the collar and bracelets turned up in Cairo."

"How do you know they were destined for Cairo?"

"If you'll recall, my sweet, Rousch had re-served himself a place on a flight from Beirut to Cairo, and he confirmed it by phone today. There are lots of wealthy Egyptians who would like to see their national trinkets back home. It's a toss-up whether Rousch would have stayed or caught the next plane out after he was paid off."

"What's going to happen to Leon?"

"He'll be extradited to the continent to face charges, along with Rousch. Il Supremo will have to find another bridge partner as well as another purser."

They were walking along again, with the brightly lit courtyard of the restaurant just ahead of them.

"Does that cross the *t*'s and dot the *i*'s for you?" he asked.

She nodded slowly. "Just one thing more—I suppose it was Leon who cut the rope at Ugarit."

"And shook us up at the villa in Iskand-erun." James nodded too. "He was familiar with both ports and had plenty of liberty to try and warn us off. If either venture had succeed-ed, it would have been reported as an accident, so he had nothing to lose. His conscience didn't bother him in the least. This evening he dared me to try and prove anything. It's a good thing we caught him in possession of the stolen items, or there wouldn't be a chance of a con-viction on any count."

A shudder went through her. "I'm glad it's over. If I'm ever approached for anything like this again, I'll run screaming in the opposite direction."

They walked on down to a corner of the restaurant wall.

"I can remember feeling like that in Venice when we started out. Now I feel like offering thanks to the gods who shoved me up the gangway of the *Lucarno*." He had been idly swinging her hand but suddenly raised it to his lips and kissed her fingertips. "Do you think now, Lisa Halliday, that we could talk about us?"

Absurd to say that a heart could beat in double time, but Lisa would have sworn that hers did and that those beats could be heard all over the Lebanese countryside. Certainly by the man beside her.

"I don't believe I have anything scheduled for the evening," she faltered, trying to keep it light.

"Good!" he bent to kiss the soft hollow of her throat. "Don't schedule anything for the next fifty years without consulting me, will you?"

"I'll want that in writing," she managed tremulously as his lips moved up to hover over hers. "I've heard what lawyers are . . ."

"Mmmm, now you're going to find out."

Then she was being kissed in the way that every woman dreams of being kissed by the man who really matters, who owns her heart and soul. Overhead, the stars and moon seemed to disappear completely as the minutes went by and they entered a heaven of their own making.

Finally Lisa pushed back breathlessly. "I didn't now it was possible to be so happy," she whispered.

"I didn't know it was possible to love anyone so much. Come back here," he pulled her to him gently, cradling her head against his chest. "You've been an elusive female long enough."

"Darling, I wasn't. I kept under your feet so much that you nearly tripped over me." She raised a laughing face. "When you weren't insulting me every other day."

"It was safer that way," he confessed. "I knew that if I once let down the bars, anything else was all off." He strove to keep his voice even. "If you're willing, we can get a special license at the embassy and be married tomorrow." There was a pause and then she felt, rather than heard, his deep chuckle. "There's not much sense in making the American taxpayers finance two cabins on the *Lucarno* when one would do."

"I had no idea you were so patriotic." She couldn't maintain that casual note either, although she sparred for time. "Something tells me this is the time to win concessions."

He pretended to consider. "There'll be a slight charge, of course. What did you have in mind?"

"Joint custody of Shadrach?"

"Agreed. No problem there." His lips traced a soft trail across her forehead.

"California oranges for breakfast?"

"We'll switch to Texas grapefruit."

"And a full-course dinner for that poor cat on the parapet if we can find him."

"We'll set him up for life, if Hany agrees." He bestowed a quizzical look. "No more Italian musclemen in the future?"

"Cross my heart. And no redheads in Florida?"

"I'll throw away my address book tonight."

They shook hands solemnly before the laughter died in his eyes to be replaced by an expression that made her heart pound. Roughly he reached out for her and pulled her into his arms again.

Lisa heard him ask unsteadily, "What do you say, my dearest? Is it a truce? Now and forever?"

Her arms tightened around him before she managed to whisper, "Truce nothing, darling, make it a victory. You've won the war!"

From the top of the wall, a straggly tomcat stared suspiciously at the two entwined figures before he went back to the chore of licking his bruised tail, still unaware of the joys his future held. And in the flower-filled courtyard, Hany glanced out at the merged shadows, shrugged philosophically, and went to take the mutton out of the oven. Love was wonderful, but there was no point in ruining dinner.